KATALIN STREET

MAGDA SZABÓ (1917–2007) was born into an old Protestant family in Debrecen, Hungary's "Calvinist Rome," on the eastern side of the great Hungarian plain. Szabó, whose father taught her to converse with him in Latin, German, English, and French, attended the University of Debrecen, studying Latin and Hungarian, and went on to work as a teacher throughout the German and Soviet occupations of Hungary in 1944 and 1945. In 1947, she published two volumes of poetry, *Bárány* (The Lamb) and *Vissza az emberig* (Return to Man), for which she received the Baumgarten Prize in 1949. Under Communist rule, the prize was repealed and her work was banned, and Szabó turned to writing fiction. Her first novel, *Freskó* (Fresco), came out in 1958, followed closely by *Az őz* (The Fawn). In 1959 she won the József Attila Prize, after which she went on to write many more novels, among them *Katalin utca* (*Katalin Street*, 1969), *Ókút* (The Ancient Well, 1970), *Régimódi történet* (An Old-Fashioned Tale, 1971), and *Az ajtó* (*The Door*, 1987). Szabó also wrote verse for children, plays, short stories, and nonfiction, including a tribute to her husband, Tibor Szobotka, a writer and translator who died in 1982. A member of the European Academy of Sciences and a warden of the Calvinist Theological Seminary in Debrecen, Szabó died in the city in which she was born, a book in her hand.

LEN RIX is a poet, critic, and former literature professor who has translated six books by Antal Szerb, including the novel *Journey by Moonlight* (available as an NYRB Classic) and, most recently, *The Martian's Guide to Budapest*. In 2006 he was awarded the Oxford-Weidenfeld Translation Prize for his translation of Magda Szabó's *The Door* (also available as an NYRB Classic), which was one of *The New York Times Book Review*'s ten best books of 2015.

OTHER BOOKS BY MAGDA SZABÓ
PUBLISHED BY NYRB CLASSICS

The Door
Translated by Len Rix
Introduction by Ali Smith

Iza's Ballad
Translated and with an introduction by George Szirtes

KATALIN STREET

MAGDA SZABÓ

Translated from the Hungarian by
LEN RIX

NEW YORK REVIEW BOOKS

New York

THIS IS A NEW YORK REVIEW BOOK
PUBLISHED BY THE NEW YORK REVIEW OF BOOKS
435 Hudson Street, New York, NY 10014
www.nyrb.com

The translation of the book was subsidized by the Hungarian Books and
Translations Office of the Petőfi Literary Museum.

PETŐFI
LITERARY
MUSEUM

HUNGARIAN BOOKS
AND TRANSLATIONS
OFFICE

Library of Congress Cataloging-in-Publication Data
Names: Szabó, Magda, 1917–2007, author. | Rix, L. B. (Leonard B.), translator.
Title: Katalin Street / by Magda Szabó ; translated by Len Rix.
Other titles: Katalin Utca. English
Description: New York : New York Review Books, 2017. | Series: New York
  Review Books Classics
Identifiers: LCCN 2017008653 (print) | LCCN 2017008880 (ebook) | ISBN
  9781681371528 (paperback) | ISBN 9781681371535 (epub)
Subjects: | BISAC: FICTION / Family Life. | FICTION / War & Military.
  | FICTION / Historical.
Classification: LCC PH3351.S592 K313 2017 (print) | LCC PH3351.S592
  (ebook) | DDC 894/.51133—dc23
LC record available at https://lccn.loc.gov/2017008653

ISBN 978-1-68137-152-8
Available as an electronic book; ISBN 978-1-68137-153-5

Printed in the United States of America on acid-free paper.
10 9 8 7 6 5 4 3 2 1

CONTENTS

THE PROCESS of growing old bears little resemblance to the way it is presented, either in novels or in works of medical science.

No work of literature, and no doctor, had prepared the former residents of Katalin Street for the fierce light that old age would bring to bear on the shadowy, barely sensed corridor down which they had walked in the earlier decades of their lives, or the way it would rearrange their memories and their fears, overturning their earlier moral judgments and system of values. They knew they should expect certain biological changes: that the body would set about its work of demolition with the same meticulous attention to detail that from the moment of conception it had applied to the task of preparing itself for the journey ahead. They had accepted that there would be alterations in their appearance and a weakening of the senses, along with changes in their tastes, their habits, and their needs; that they might fall prey to gluttony or lose all interest in food, become fear-ridden or hypersensitive and fractious. They had resigned themselves to the prospect of increasing difficulties with digestion and sleeping, things they had taken for granted when young, like life itself. But no one had told them that the most frightening thing of all about the loss of youth is not what is taken away but what is granted in exchange. Not wisdom. Not serenity. Not sound judgment or tranquility. Only the awareness of universal disintegration.

There came too the realization that advancing age had taken the past, which in childhood and early maturity had seemed to them so firmly rounded off and neatly parceled up, and ripped it open. Everything that had happened was still there, right up to the present, but now suddenly different. Time had shrunk to specific moments, important events to single episodes, familiar places to the mere backdrop to individual scenes, so that, in the end, they understood that of everything that had made up their lives thus far only one or two places, and a handful of moments, really mattered. Everything else was just so much wadding around their fragile existences, wood shavings stuffed into a trunk to protect the contents on the long journey to come.

They had discovered too that the difference between the living and the dead is merely qualitative, that it doesn't count for much. And they had learned that in everyone's life there is only one person whose name can be cried out in the moment of death.

PLACES

NONE OF them had ever got used to the apartment or grown to like it. They just put up with it, as with so many other things.

It was the place that sheltered them from the rain and the heat of the sun, nothing more: a cave, if slightly more comfortable than a cave. An air of neglect hung over everything, defying the best efforts of Mrs. Elekes to keep it clean. Hopelessly untidy herself, any semblance of order or homeliness she might impose would be short-lived, evaporating within minutes under the influence of some mysterious force that followed her around. The glass selected at random by a guest would always be the one she had given the most cursory wiping over, or failed to wash at all. A man reaching round for an ashtray would invariably light upon one overflowing with ash and cigarette stubs, which she had forgotten to empty.

The apartment was on the sixth floor of a relatively new block on the left bank of the Danube, with views across the river. From its windows they could see their old house. Its façade had been covered in scaffolding for several months now, undergoing redevelopment along with its immediate neighbors. It looked like a childhood friend who, either in anger or a spirit of fun, had put on a mask and forgotten to take it off long after the party had ended. Bálint, Irén, and

Mrs. Elekes would often linger on the balcony, staring across the river, even after more houses had been built along the embankment. But if either Mr. Elekes or Kinga joined them, they would immediately turn away and pretend to have some particular business there.

Living in the apartment depressed them profoundly—so many flights of stairs to climb, the rooms so tiny!—and they desperately missed their garden. Besides, they all had personal sources of grief, Mr. Elekes in particular. Apart from his granddaughter, Kinga, everyone was extremely attentive to him. It was as if, with the coming of maturity, they had taken to heart all those injunctions about the virtuous life that he had showered on his former pupils, and they enveloped his days in a wearying solicitude. With his formidable strength of will he had learned to look after himself. He had always enjoyed educational handicrafts, so he made paper bags and boxes for a cooperative, and he worked away on his type-writer—short articles on pedagogic problems tapped out with two fingers. From time to time Irén would announce that she had sent one of them off to an important educational journal and it had been accepted. He never commented. He knew perfectly well that his articles had nothing new to say, certainly nothing of relevance in the present climate, and that these supposed honoraria, pitiful as they were, had been taken from the housekeeping money. The notes would be placed in his hand for him to touch and promptly returned whence they came.

The furniture was all from their former home, with one or two exceptions. A great many pieces had had to be sold off when they moved, to fit the smaller space. Mr. Elekes continued to sit beneath the bust of Cicero, quite why, he was no longer sure, since the contents of the desk and its drawers were now Irén's. Twice a day he would be taken out for a walk, as you would a dog. But despite his longing for the smell of the sun, the wind, and the water, he was always conscious that the person taking him was short of time and had rather more important things to do than trudge along at a snail's pace with him beside the Danube, and soon he would politely ask to be taken home. When Irén took him out she always bought him a little treat—in the summer an ice cream or roasted ear of corn, in winter a slice of baked pumpkin or some hot chestnuts. Whatever it was, he nibbled at it with loathing and impotent shame.

He was the only one who had any patience with little Kinga. She was always getting in people's way and no one else had time to waste on her, so it totally demoralized her when he too could no longer see what she was doing, even when she stuck her tongue out at him or made the donkey-ears sign at passersby from the balcony. He had no status in her eyes: she was far too sure of his affection and felt no need to strive for it. It was Bálint that she attacked with her sentimental effusions. But he never returned her affection. He would tell her, rather sharply, to go and find her father, and not to forget that she was Pali's daughter, not his.

Meanwhile Mrs. Elekes floundered despairingly in an ocean of dishwater. Irén and Pali occupied two of the rooms in the apartment and it was all too much for her. It drove her to her wit's end. On the one hand, given her lack of strength and energy, the apartment was dauntingly large; on the other, compared with the house in Katalin Street it was mean and cramped, and she was deeply ashamed of it. Moving through the rooms she was permanently conscious of the absence of objects and items of furniture that had either been disposed of or had simply disappeared. Deprived of her attic, her basement, and her larder with its built-in cupboards and drawers, she would sometimes collapse in total bewilderment, a monument of impotence.

She missed her daughter Blanka too, so much so that on days when a long-expected letter failed to arrive she would curl up in misery. She would stand in the narrow entrance to greet the postman with a look that made him lower his eyes, as if it were his fault that the stupid envelope the old woman had been hoping for hadn't come. She thought of Blanka more and more often, with an ever more desperate longing, and she increasingly dreaded the moment when Irén would finish work and arrive home.

They all dreaded it, even Mr. Elekes. He might not be able to see what was happening, but he was always aware of his daughter's return, coming in, greeting the others—how exhausted she was, what a difficult day she'd had at school— and immediately setting about putting things in order, like a robot. Mr. Elekes, Bálint, and Kinga would watch in silence as she made her way from room to room, straightening a book here, repositioning a vase there. Her mother, who felt she had already worn herself to death over the housework, often longed to snatch up the tablecloth and throw it and everything on it out of the window. The silent daily warfare over the table, the library, the precise distance between two objects that she had never mastered in all these years was infuriating and humiliating.

But when Irén began to shout, their reactions were very different. Mr. Elekes listened to the raised voice, the altered, unnatural tone, with a deep sense of shame. His wife, almost beside herself with terror, racked her brains to think how they might have offended her. Bálint simply watched with interest. Seeing the expression on his face, standing in a corner smoking and gazing at her with something close to amusement, always stopped her in her tracks. She would instantly change her tone, often bursting into tears and apologizing to everyone, always with the same refrain: she was getting old, she was exhausted, her nerves were in shreds. Her lack of self-control, her shouting, gesticulating, kicking off her slippers, and her constant complaining were in fact more upsetting than even Blanka's former sins. From Blanka, after all, her father had always expected some sort of delinquency or base conduct, if not quite everything that happened later.

Kinga, who had never known Irén to be any different, listened in amazement when her grandparents talked about their former home and her mother's childhood. The Irén who supervised her homework was the mother she knew— even if one who seemed permanently surprised that this little girl was actually hers—and that Irén showed small resemblance to the wonderful personage who shone so brightly in the old people's reminiscences.

Bálint, when he found himself in the apartment, was bored and bewildered most of the time. It was a constant source of surprise to him how little difference it made that he now lived here, and how vain had been the hope that by marrying Irén he could escape the unreality of his life. The number of items that Mrs. Elekes had saved from his former home was small. There were several ornaments and objects from her former home too, but none of them conjured up the magic he had been hoping for. Irén's new abode had turned out to be nothing like the one in Katalin Street, and even here he was haunted by the sense of being *somewhere else*. The marriage to Irén had showed him that she yearned and pined for Katalin Street just as much as he did, that she had not found it, and neither had her parents, who were locked in the same hopeless quest to recover it. Only Kinga lived without expectation, in cheerful innocence, not forever yearning for the voice of some long-lost person. She knew nothing of the world beyond this apartment in Budapest, and reminiscences that had no bearing on herself she thought both dishonest and stupid.

This tyranny of *somewhere else* was a cruel one. It stopped Bálint from seeing both the reality that existed and what he would have liked that reality to be. During his prison days, for example, while he was waiting to be transferred to the medical service, he had noticed only the hospital wards and the university teaching facility, drawing a veil over the barbed wire and the blinding floodlights. Then, once he had been sent there, he would suddenly stop in the middle of his assigned duties and stare in wonder at his filthy hands—how could he be expected to handle his patients with fingers like these?—or ask himself why he was sitting in a lecture room dressed in such extraordinary clothes. On the other hand, however desperately he tried to conjure up images of his former life, he could never visualize the Held family garden, the row of riding saddles belonging to his father, the Major, or the bust of Cicero in its place in the Elekeses' house. On his release, whether as a lodger now in their new apartment or at his place of work, he was barely conscious of the room he was in, the bathtub in which he sat, the patients he treated, or the comfortable bed in which he lay at night—he saw only what spoke to him of his prison days. When he administered injections, it felt like driving a fork into the ground. Even when there was no one else in the apartment, he would rush to finish what he was doing in the bathroom because the time allowed in the latrines was strictly limited. When he might have been sleeping peacefully in his bed, he would be startled awake by the summons of the prison bell. While Katalin Street remained partly as it had been and Irén was still living in her old house before the social rehousing scheme took it over, the strangers who now occupied the other two didn't seem to mind his staring in through the window of his former home. But he stared in vain. The house, though it still stood seemingly unchanged and palpable to touch, had effectively vanished. And with it the entire street, though he could still walk down it. Everything had gone—as lightly as if someone had plucked a handkerchief from his coat pocket.

Even during his time in the village—that most harmonious period of his adult life—he had been unable to conjure up what he most yearned for. The principle of *somewhere else* still toyed with him. His house stood on its own plot of land, but in his mind he was still in that rented room on busy Rákóczi Street, and that room, rather than his new home, was what he saw all around him. As evening drew in, knowing that music would upset the landlord, he would turn the radio down and sit there, among the furniture he had inherited from Blanka—it seemed to cringe in fear—listening intently to the silence and the typical dusk-to-dawn sounds of the village. And now, living with Irén, everything—the prison and the hospital, the rented room in Rákóczi Street, his time in Blanka's apartment and the house in the village—coexisted in the same time frame. He would smile to see the women struggling to maintain order in this surreal stage set of a place, where strange scenes and locations came and went. What was the point of polishing the door handles when it was all bare earth, barbed wire, and blinding floodlights, and anyway there weren't any handles, just a guard standing there . . . and why wax the parquet floor when there were only stone slabs in the hospital, it was ridiculous trying to make them shine . . . and what were they doing now, messing about in the bathroom: didn't they know that prisoners weren't allowed there? But of course there was no bathroom . . . and why all this fuss about the balcony and the flower boxes? The landlord had expressly forbidden them, and besides, anything in a pot would rapidly come to grief in Blanka's care . . . and why were there all these people in his little house: he'd always lived on his own there . . . and look, that little girl seems to have wandered in: she must have been left behind after this morning's clinic. . . .

Scenes of his former life drifted in and out of his bedroom door. When he was too tired to read or listen to music and had nothing else to do, he would lean back in his chair in the corner where Blanka once cocooned herself and simply watch the ever-changing procession. He would have rather liked to greet its members. He wanted to ask them if they knew each other as well as he knew them.

The actual reason why he was in the apartment at all, the reason why he had sought Irén out at that exhibition—the one episode that he could recall in every detail, that he knew as intimately as his own body and central nervous system— never appeared in the procession, either with Irén present or without her. Nothing in their daily conversations or recollections ever brought it back. Irén, it was clear, knew the password no more than he did. He had married her to no purpose. The old Katalin Street on the other side of the river was gone forever. So too were the Held families, the Major, Mrs. Temes, and Henriette.

In their free time, if they weren't going out and there were no visitors, they sat and talked. Their visitors were few because every time Irén had guests it was a particular trial for the old people: it meant that they went to bed later than they liked, or if they did go at their usual time, they would be constantly woken by the comings and goings and noises from the kitchen late at night when Irén washed the glasses and put them away. It was at times like these that they felt most painfully that everything of their old home was gone: the Katalin Street they once lived in had been carried off by a bird to some never-never land. Now they would all have to accommodate themselves to an adult Irén who, for her part, had neither the time nor the inclination to adapt her present self to their wishes.

They often sat together and talked as a family. Mr. Elekes would perch stiffly on his seat, all attention, while his wife flopped exhausted in an armchair. Kinga would cuddle up against Bálint to watch the others in fascination. She found their voices irresistibly funny. Everyone spoke as if Elekes were deaf: loud-ly and ve-ry clear-ly. It amused her intensely. For the old man it was almost more than he could bear. In fact, most of the time the irritation was universal and mutual. They sat together and talked because they simply couldn't live without each other.

The moment Pali first saw Irén in Bálint's company—it was after he had married her—he realized how futile it would be to stay stumbling around in a daze among these people. They shared some private knowledge that he didn't—he and little Kinga. They were party to a secret from which he was forever excluded. When Irén finally sent him packing, of all their friends and acquaintances he was the only one who understood why she had done so, the only one who wasn't shocked and outraged that she had "traded him in" for a man who had no future, was generally considered an incompetent doctor who had fallen into his profession by mistake, was not particularly attractive, was visibly older than Irén, transparently not in the grip of some wild passion for her, and had already left her once before for someone else—as Irén herself had told him. He knew that this wasn't about Irén and Bálint, or about himself and Irén. It was about something he couldn't put his finger on—something that bound these people together. They tossed coded words at one another in a kind of ball game, allusions incomprehensible to himself and to his child that made their eyes light up and left old Elekes tittering with amusement. Once Pali had overcome his sense of insult and hurt he was simply glad to be able to go without guilt, to be able to "leave them to it," playing their weird family games by themselves, behind closed doors.

But even when they did manage to evoke the secret world they shared, the heightened spirits and raised voices never lasted long. The performance quickly exhausted them. The game had no resolution, it brought no release, like desire aroused but not followed by a full embrace. They were too few to support the weight of the images their words conjured up from the void; they ached with longing for the dead, and the mood in the room started to sag, seemed to press down on their heads, like a collapsed ceiling. Before long, they would realize it was pointless—but all too soon they were at it again, because they still hadn't come to terms with it. They hoped that if they clung to one another and held one another's hands, and if they could hit upon the right words, then perhaps they might find their way out of the labyrinth and somehow make their way home. And until that happened they would have to endure this unreal, impermanent abode in the sky, so close to the water. Even a bird needs somewhere to perch and rest. There were four of them making the journey, perhaps five—Blanka was still alive, and she still wrote occasionally. If just one of them could find the way back, then they all would. Mr. Elekes would recover his sight and lead the way. Mrs. Elekes would slowly relax, she would put on weight, become idle again, and start to sew cushions. Irén and Bálint would rediscover their old love, and Irén would grow gentle, soft-spoken, a fairy child once again. The sun would once more shine out of Bálint. His confidence would return, and with it the prospect of a great medical career.

Henriette was with them on one of these occasions. She did not assume a physical form that they could see, but she was there. She listened in sorrow. She knew that without the ones who had died their quest was in vain: they would never find their way back to Katalin Street. Kinga was still a small child at this time, and she saw Henriette. But when she tried to explain that there was someone else in the room, she simply wasn't believed. Her grandfather recited a rhyme about naughty little girls, and Irén gave her a slap on the hand and told her not to tell fibs, it wasn't nice, then picked her up and took her off to bed.

THE HOUSE stood at the tip of the promontory, high above the reach of the waves, but the sea was audible throughout the long day, sometimes just a murmur, sometimes much louder. If you gazed out over the garden wall it was visible all around, ceaselessly hurling itself against the rocks as if it had some eternal score to settle with the edge of the land.

Blanka's sleep was never entirely unbroken, but in summer she was often awake all night. She found the heat intolerable. Her husband, her mother-in-law, and the servants took this in their stride, allowing her to sleep all day, whenever and for as long as she wished, and even when she wandered restlessly about the house, refusing food, they made due allowance. When the Dog Star raged she would pace back and forth in a thin nightdress, until either her husband or her mother-in-law found her "almost naked," and insisted she put on a dressing gown. They knew that as soon as the heat abated she would calm down and be her old self again, gentle and amenable.

For example, she faithfully observed the Sunday dress code. This greatly endeared her to her mother-in-law, who knew what a sacrifice it was for her, in the intense heat, to don the traditional island costume for women attending church, sweltering inside her black robes and black head scarf purely to please the family. The demands Blanka made on them were so few that they readily forgave her erratic behavior in the summer and waited patiently for her to recover her usual self. If they noticed her becoming abnormally restless, they too stayed up all night—not a great sacrifice on an island where people often kept irregular hours: the day would start earlier and end later than elsewhere, and between noon and early evening life came to a complete standstill. During this time her husband and his mother would sit together and chat; the old lady would nibble at sweet pastries, the husband would mix himself drinks, and the housemaid went about under the slowly turning fan picking up items of clothing that Blanka had cast off at random around the room, or take a pair of slippers out into the garden for her if she had gone out barefoot. After that she would sit herself down at her employers' feet, on the bottom stair of the marble staircase, and watch her mistress's comings and goings with genuine curiosity. She adored Blanka, who had shown her more kindness and simple humanity than anyone in her life. She watched the way Blanka would stand at the end of the garden, gazing out in all directions. She felt so sorry for the girl that she regularly prayed for her.

Sometimes Blanka would tear her dressing gown open so that she could feel the cool breath of the sea air on her skin, thus exposing her breasts. Her husband would immediately shout at her. Startled, she would quickly button herself up again and fan her face vigorously, panting all the while. The family felt just a little hurt by her failure to adapt to their climate. She had learned their language quickly, spoke it flawlessly, almost elegantly, and had even adopted their religion—surely a far more difficult thing to do than putting up with the summer heat? They sometimes saw her walk the length of the stone-floored rooms—there were no doors separating them—then go into the kitchen and take a handful of ice cubes from the huge refrigerator. She never put them in drinks. Instead she would take them out into the garden and play a game, sliding them along her arms and down her neck or balancing them on her head.

If they noticed her nodding off, they would go and bring her in. She often fell asleep beside the garden wall. She never sat on a bench, only on the ground, under some fragrant trees, from where she had to be led, half supported, back to the house.

Her mother-in-law's eyes always followed her with interest and affection. It was impossible for her not to love Blanka. She was so biddable, so fundamentally different from anyone she knew, and she showed her so much more respect than any of the uppity local girls ever did, having none of their modern ideas about life. If you said you didn't want her to go outside, she would simply stay indoors. Never in all her time among her compatriots had the old lady come across such a refined young woman as her daughter-in-law, who never undertook any kind of useful task, apparently felt no obligation to do so, and seemed formed by nature to be loving and submissive. The only thing that troubled her with regard to Blanka was her failure so far to bless them with grandchildren, but she hoped that sooner or later the girl would bring them that supreme joy. After all, her son had married her only recently.

So they tolerated her irregular nocturnal behavior, and her husband, though he felt the sacrifice keenly, accepted her absence from the marital bed in summer. When he found he could no longer contain himself, he would fall asleep immediately afterward. Sated and exhausted, he never knew how Blanka would then waken from her near-stupor and lie fully awake, her eyes open, her body tense, her mind filled with sadness, before going out to the bathroom and letting the water from the shower pour over her until she was shivering with cold.

During the embrace, her mind was elsewhere, unlike her husband who gave himself up to it in ecstasy. She would note how oddly their sweating bodies stuck to each other or the way their skin made little squelching noises. But she felt nothing: only the intense heat, despite the fans humming overhead. No matter how much water she drank, her only source of relief was to lie quite motionless, or better still, to leave the bed and go outside into the garden and crouch down beyond the wall, fanned by the breeze from the sea.

In summer, things were of course easier during the day. After an especially disturbed night she would sleep soundly, or, if she grew tired of lying in bed, she would go down to the sea and swim for hours. The thing about the local climate she found hardest to adapt herself to was that the temperature never dropped during the night, and the long periods of wakefulness she endured as a result brought back memories that at first she had no wish to recall. Only later, once she realized that the more she tried to fend them off the more obstinately they returned to torment her, did she stop resisting them. Had she not been so lovable and submissive, and had people on the island—a place that had witnessed the birth of gods—not seen so many strange and wonderful things, her lot might have been more difficult. But her husband was devoted to her, and her mother-in-law's sympathy made her position in the house absolutely secure.

The old lady loved her perhaps even more than her husband did. To an outsider this would have seemed all the more surprising, for, notwithstanding her willingness to submit to instruction like a child—obedient in everything that was asked of her, wearing the traditional costume for church attendance and the visiting and receiving of guests simply to please her mother-in-law, and even adopting their faith— she was still an outsider, a complete stranger. But it made no difference. She was accepted as she was, in appearance so like those other women from abroad who alone had been able to redirect her son's love onto themselves—for he, sadly, had never been attracted by the girls of his own country. The old lady knew that those foreign women, arriving on their yachts with their pet dogs kenneled in their cabins, were rich and drank too much. They would mock her and ridicule her ancient customs; they would oppose her in everything and turn her son against her. So she had welcomed Blanka. Blanka had the same long legs and blond hair of those other fair women from the West, but she was homeless, penniless, and humble. So everyone had cause for satisfaction—her son who had attained his exotic ideal, and she who had gained a daughter-in-law who deferred to her in everything.

The house was surrounded by palm trees, laurel, myrtle, and ancient oleanders, and the steps leading up to the entrance, the open sitting area, and the inner courtyard were lined with dwarf varieties in majolica pots. The old lady had been much amused to hear that Blanka's family back home had a collection of cacti, tiny plants that they struggled to keep alive. In response, so that here too she might have a cactus of her own, her husband had carved her name into the trunk of one that had grown into a tree. There were more smiles when they learned that her family had to bring the oleander into the house in winter to save it from freezing. Blanka would go and stand beside her new cactus and carve words of her own into the thick fleshy leaves, though neither

her husband nor his mother, who were familiar with and able to read the Latin script, could understand their meaning in the foreign tongue. When they asked what she had written, she replied: just names. This won their respect. It pleased them that she was loyal, that she treasured her memories. When All Souls' Day came round on the island they gave her a bundle of tall thin candles, as was the local tradition, to make an offering to her own far-distant dead. They were surprised and impressed by the number she lit (so many of her loved ones must have died!), and by the length of time she spent at the altar. But this too pleased the old lady. Once she herself had passed away, the girl would surely cherish her own memory in like fashion.

The mother-in-law was less pleased on those days (though there were rather fewer of them) when she was more active; but they forgave her them too. Blanka was always more alive in the winter. When her husband was away, at his office in the town or in court, everyone was surprised and intrigued to see her suddenly busy. Even the menservants would steal into the house to observe her from behind a pillar. Sitting at her husband's desk! It was most unsuitable. The mother-in-law gave them strict instructions not to tell anyone.

On a shelf above the desk stood a white bust of the Greek father-in-law. From time to time she would sit down beneath it, take up her husband's legal documents (of which she understood not a word), draw a series of lines across a piece of paper, and study them intently. Henriette, who often visited the island, knew that the bust stood for the one of Cicero in Katalin Street: Blanka was playing at being her father, marking his pupils' essays. Reading the words carved into the giant cactus, Henriette had noted that all their names were there, including her own. She had also seen the number of candles Blanka had lit on the altar of the dead, not just for her own family and for the Major but for everyone she had left behind, even the Biró family governess, Mrs. Temes.

Henriette was often present in the room with her. She was curious to know which of them Blanka remembered, and in what way. It fascinated her, watching her down among the low-slung chairs and bronze-footed sofas, playing at being those people. The husband's study might have been off-limits to her as a woman, but it was the only room that was anything like the ones she had been brought up in. In the kitchen—where again she had no business to be—the servants watched in awe as she burst into unwonted activity. Like all the girls taught by Mrs. Temes, she could cook superbly. At home she had been too lazy to make the effort, and here she thought of involving herself only when moved by a wish to explore her memories and to re-create Mrs. Temes's presence around her: the old, familiar smells quickly brought her back. Blanka was, however, the only one who actually enjoyed eating what she had prepared: anyone else who tried it would push the plate away, complaining that she had brutally overdone the spice, and that simply tasting it had given them a stomach ache.

The person Blanka most often played at being was her mother. So she sewed cushions, enormous productions covered in mysterious symbols, that ended up being given away to the servants. The servants had no idea what to do with them either. No one on the island ever put cushions on chairs (it was simply too hot) and they would discreetly "disappear." The strange motifs that Blanka had so carefully embroidered on them did attract attention: people stared at the picture she made of a Hungarian swing well without the least idea of what it might possibly represent. It was the same with the Chain Bridge over the Danube, drawn from memory and stitched with blue thread. The image meant nothing to them. Unlike the famous lions. A god had once lived on the island in the form of a lion. Perhaps this chain bridge also stood for something sacred?

The family looked on with a mixture of interest, curiosity, and bafflement at the way she walked too—shoulders pulled back, knees stiff, body as straight as a ramrod. They had no way of knowing that this was how the officer class of a certain period had once held and carried themselves.

Blanka even learned to play the island's musical instruments. When visitors came, and the old lady wanted to show off her gentle, amenable daughter-in-law—not like the local wenches, all of them so uppity and self-willed, dolling themselves up in the fashions of the distant capital and pouring scorn on their elders—to the other old ladies, she was always happy to oblige. She would breathe soft airs on her pipe, much admired; and the songs she gave them—taught to her by Mrs. Held, who had loved playing pentatonic melodies on her piano—were pronounced the strangest in the world.

On these occasions Henriette, listening in the brightly lit, incense-laden salon, with the servants bringing a steady supply of coffee and refreshments, felt her own mother's presence far more strongly than anywhere else. The sinuous, faltering, childlike tunes seemed to echo from the walls of the house in Katalin Street. Blanka's stories about the past brought back a sense of her father too. The Greek husband had built up a fine library during his student days in Paris: it included a collection of foreign-language books, and since arriving on the island Blanka had taken to reading. "Why don't you ever read proper literature?" Mr. Held had often asked, urging the classics upon her. She had always fled, laughing, before turning around and shouting, "Because they're boring! I'm not interested." Blanka's father found this a source of deep shame, but what point could there be in trying to get her to read when no one else in the family, apart from Irén, ever did? Now, all Mr. Held's favorite books were there in front of her, in French translation . . . and there too, moving among them, was Henriette's father himself, nodding approval and smiling. She watched as his hand reached out to take one down from a shelf and place it on the table. They used the same system of classification here that had been followed at home, and the great works were aligned on the shelves in the old familiar order.

Henriette was deeply moved to discover how persistently Blanka's thoughts turned to her. For example, in the course of his studies abroad the husband had observed the peculiar fondness that people over there had for animals, but his mother, who had been born on the island and had left it only once to visit a monastery on the mainland, had not. So she looked on in some astonishment when Blanka began tending to the local strays. There were packs of them, all over the island, with not a soul to care for or show the slightest concern for them, alive or dead. If Blanka came across a mule or a donkey tormented by flies or bleeding from the mouth, she would immediately order the servants, "Get her something to drink, clean her up, and let her out of that harness." This behavior was yet another source of pride to her husband, even if his mother couldn't possibly understand. He knew that this was how foreigners were; it showed that she was a true Westerner. He accepted her attitude without reservation and seldom showed irritation, even when he could barely make his way into his own house through a pack of strays looking for food, or move easily about his garden through the horde of Blanka's cats. However, whenever Henriette heard Blanka call to them, it was always by the same name: hers. Every stray, every hungry or diseased creature that she took in and tried to nurse was a Henriette. At the sound of that name thirsty, heat-exhausted cats and dogs with heart-melting eyes would raise their heads, and Blanka would run to them with water and make sure they drank, while her mother-in-law and the servants gazed on, at once dumb-founded and transported with admiration. A maid pointing out a dog that had been hit by a vehicle and left prostrate in the dust would use just one word: "Henriette." And Blanka would take it, in her own car, to the island's hospital where, because of the large number of foreigners who arrived in the summer, almost all bringing their pets with them, a vet from the capital was always on duty.

Blanka never played at being Bálint or Irén, but she did talk about them: in fact they were the only ones she ever spoke about much. Her mother-in-law loved the stories and never tired of hearing them, but Henriette listened in mount-ing astonishment to the transformations made in Blanka's life, the circumstances in which she had left the country, and the entire history of her family. She even had the Major as her father. As a regular visitor to the island, Henriette was not altogether surprised by this. A teacher had little standing there. A man like Blanka's husband would never defer to the headmaster of the local school but he would regularly entertain the commander of the town garrison. So in these tales Mr. Elekes and the Major became one and the same person. And since she could hardly avoid talking about her mother, to whom it was difficult to attribute much in the way of kindliness or charm, not to mention her total incapacity to maintain domestic order, Blanka had created a personage that Henriette instantly recognized as her own mother. So Mrs. Held assumed a double role on the island: Blanka would play her favorite songs, and describe in detail her person, her character, and her gentle innocence. But of Henriette and the Held family as a whole, and of Mrs. Temes, she said not a word. It was all Bálint and Irén, the young Bálint being passed off as her brother. That was much simpler than explaining what he had been in reality. On the island, to say that a girl had a boy as a friend could mean only one thing.

As for Bálint: Blanka's mother-in-law was a tough old lady, hardened by experience, who never complained about anything, but like most people of her age she suffered from various ailments. So she loved to dream of this great doctor, a professor no less, living in a faraway country, before whom no illness or condition could prevail. On the other hand, since neither she nor Blanka's husband thought it suitable that a woman should go out and earn her living, Irén, who had never done anything else, became a volunteer devoted to charitable work. She was also made out to be religious— far more so than ever in real life—in fact verging on bigotry. In a word, she became so perfect that the old lady wondered if perhaps they should help her to leave her homeland to come and marry her favorite nephew. She was already well pleased with Blanka, and this Irén seemed to be even more remarkable and irreproachable.

Listening to these stories, Henriette was astonished that no one, neither the old lady nor her son, seemed to realize that there was, or even might be, anything seriously wrong with Blanka. One incident particularly shocked her. She was back with them once again, the servants were sitting, as they so often did, at the old lady's feet on the stairs at the front of the house, and her son had just returned from his office in the town. He was still in the dark suit that he wore when conducting a trial. In the paralyzing heat the palm tree barely stirred, and the Henriettes had flopped down with their eyes closed, scarcely able to breathe. Blanka pressed her cheek against the trunk of the cactus tree and suddenly cried, "*Hó! Jég!*" ("Snow! Ice!") These were easy words to catch, and the servants took up the refrain and tossed it about among themselves, like an orange. The old lady caught it too, laughed, and shouted the words "*Hó!*" "*Jég!*" like someone cheering on a sports team. Then Blanka leaned over the seawall and screamed at the waves, "*Katalin utca! Katalin utca!*" ("Katalin Street! Katalin Street!") This was more difficult, but for just that reason they soon mastered it. "*Katalin utca! Katalin utca!*" cried her husband, as he too laughed, gazing in pride and delight that even on such a torrid afternoon his wife could entertain them with something so charming and playful. He thought she was amused by the bizarre sounds of her own mother tongue—those ridiculous words that meant nothing to anyone—and that was why the tears were streaming down her face.

HENRIETTE visited her old home regularly, and it made a lot of people envious. Not everyone was able to do this, and it left them very angry to see others free to come and go at will. At first she tried to justify herself, explaining how happy she had been at home, how even as a child she had deliberately stored up memories of the three houses and the way they had all lived there. But her arguments convinced no one, and she had given up trying. She had the impression that some of her companions saw her in much the same way as the Soldier had, by the blue light of his electric torch. What made the thought all the more disturbing was that he had arrived in that place not long after she had, and he seemed to be always hovering close at hand. She found this almost unbearable at first, and it never really ceased to make her nervous. The first time they met she had been so terrified she started to run. Only after some time did she realize that there was nothing more he could do to her now, and besides, he clearly had no hostile intentions.

They met frequently. She came to understand why he stared at her all the time and followed her around. He had forgotten everything. Her face was the only thing that had stayed with him, this one face that so frightened and disturbed him but also—in his unbearable loneliness—drew him irresistibly to it, the face of the only person he knew.

He spoke to her often. He would lie down in front of her, his chin resting on his hands. Gazing up at her from this position he would beg her to tell him how he could get back to his lost family. She, who was always going back and forth, who spent time both in her old home and visiting her friends, surely she would know how it was done? Henriette never answered. She simply fled to avoid seeing him. She was the only one who could point him on his way, but she never did, however much he begged her.

No one oversaw the amount of time she spent away. Not even her parents asked where she was going. From the moment she arrived she had been left to work out the rules and customs of the place entirely by herself. This was a miserable experience, because all her life Mr. and Mrs. Held had helped her find her way around. The discovery that nothing here was as she had imagined depressed her for a long time. Her first meeting with her parents—that moment she had so often looked forward to in her thoughts—had been truly dreadful. They made no attempt to explain what sort of world it was that she would henceforth be living in. It was the first time since her childhood that they had failed to give her advice, or, rather, had failed even to consider that she might need any. They had been expecting her, but she had the feeling that her arrival had simply been an embarrassment to them, and a painful one at that. They were no longer together. They had separated, and both were now living with their own parents. When Henriette presented herself, Mrs. Held became childish and frivolous, and Mr. Held sniffled and whimpered about some ridiculous trifle. In fact she hadn't recognized them: it was they who greeted her. Between the joy of seeing her again and the feeling of distress at their altered state, neither parent thought that some sort of explanation might be due to her.

The constant transformation that both her parents were capable of was so bizarre and so disconcerting that it made her want never again to be with them, or at least not as often as before, and after a few further attempts she gave up seeking their company.

When they spoke to her, they did so as the parents she had known, but if their own parents came looking for them, or if they wanted to be with their parents, they would instantly change and become noisy and boisterous. Mr. Held, once so quiet and reserved in his speech, would begin to grizzle and fret, or shriek with laughter and gabble nonsense; upon which her grandfather, whom Henriette would in normal circumstances have been delighted to see, would seize him by the wrists and swing him around until he squealed with joy. Whenever Mrs. Held saw her own parents approaching she would immediately push Henriette away and start to yell "Mummy, Mummy!" clapping her hands and spinning around. Sometimes she would squat down, cover her face with her hands, and peer up at them through her fingers, giggling all the while at her own cleverness.

Everyone who arrived in this place as mature adults—as married couples and the parents of children—was subject to these changes of form that Henriette found so unbearable. She knew she was being unjust but she found them hard to forgive. She also noticed that her mother's visits when homesick were not always to Katalin Street but often to the house she had grown up in; and that likewise her father visited his own childhood home, in a different town, calling on people she had never met, and this made her very sad, in fact jealous. She got over it in time, and instead of seeking them out she simply withdrew. She had noticed that of all the adults she knew only the Soldier was childless, and his appearance never changed: his face and his personality, unlike those of everyone else, were always the same. So she avoided him, her own parents, and the other adults, preferring to visit her old home instead.

She reconstructed it piece by piece. Then, because they had both been an integral part of her life since the age of six, she did the same to the Elekes and Biró family homes, and on to the entire street from the church to the site of the old Turkish well that had been destroyed by a bomb during the war and was now a long-distance coach stop. The Elekeses' and the Birós' houses, like hers, had been joined together to create a social housing block and the three gardens merged to form a little park with benches and wide umbrellas for the old people to sit in the shade beneath—a sight that came as a shock to Henriette on her first visit. The separate gardens were now a continuous lawn around which beds of drought-resistant flowers stared blankly. The faces of the old people looked equally dried out, but at least they were alert. Almost all were focused on a window in one of the rooms at the back of the block, where a nurse was leaning out, gazing at the sky, and completely ignoring them. "This isn't right," she told herself. "Something's wrong here. Why does no one tell them?" She stood there for a while, waiting. Perhaps the nurse would see her and call down to the elderly residents: "Look! Once there were young people living here, and joy and health and good cheer!" But of course nothing of the kind happened.

Sitting on one of the benches was Mrs. Temes, mumbling unintelligibly to herself. Henriette watched her suddenly draw her body up and slyly help herself to a biscuit from the open tin belonging to the person beside her, whose eyes were fixed on the nurse at the window. Henriette was so horrified that she fled the scene. This time she created her own Katalin Street. There was no coach stop and, in the space between the Turkish well and the church, the social housing block was replaced by three open gates, side by side: the Elekeses', her own, and the Birós'. She passed through the one in the middle, and found herself, at long last, standing in front of the home she had been pining for.

The moment she arrived inside the house she would hear the sound of her father's drill. It had never frightened her: she knew it was the source of their livelihood. She had always thought of it as a kind of pet animal that was there on guard to let everyone know the family was at home. She passed through the entrance hall and the waiting area, greeting the patients as she went, and on into the surgery. She wasn't allowed in there when her father was working, but she opened the door so quietly that neither he nor the person he was treating was aware of her presence. She stood there watching him, as he leaned over the patient with a mirror and promised him, "Now this won't hurt." She never spoke to him. She simply wanted to reassure herself that he really was there. Then she closed the door and went to look for her mother.

Sometimes she would find her in the kitchen, leaning over bottles of sugar and jam and enveloped in a sweet fragrance. Or she would be in the salon, reading or singing, accompanying herself on the piano, or ironing her husband's white shirts. With her too Henriette spent only a few moments on these visits, just long enough to reassure herself that her mother really was there and was still unaware that any other form of life might be possible. Each time she gently touched her face, her hair, or her hand, then pushed her away and gazed for ages at her own fingers, still warm from the body they had caressed. "You really shouldn't do that, Henriette," her mother would say, and then laugh.

Comforted, she would leave her and continue on through the rooms she hadn't yet seen. In the bedroom she would open the wardrobe to make sure nothing was missing, take out a few towels, then put them back. In the morning room she made sure her mother's sewing table was still in place. In her father's office she restored the works of classical literature to an upright position and arranged them in the correct order. In the salon she always looked for the footstool tucked beneath the sofa: she seemed to think it might not be there, which for some reason always bothered her, and when she found it, with its gold-framed Gobelin-style tapestry depicting a shepherd and shepherdess standing on opposite banks of the stream—he with cap in hand to greet her, she with a jug and a beribboned stick in her hand— Henriette was all nodding approval.

In the kitchen she peeped into the sideboard. It always gratified her to see the number of saucepans they had—though why did they need so many? Once she had assured herself that everything was in order she moved on to her bedroom to start her homework: she knew she wouldn't be allowed to go to the Elekeses or the Birós until she had finished it.

She had almost reached the end when Mr. Held, his last patient having left, came to see how far she had got. She showed him her vocabulary list and he corrected it without recourse to a dictionary. "He always comes to my rescue," she thought. "He knows everything. He always knows how to do things. What would happen to me if one day he wasn't here?" She stood up and pressed herself against him. This signified the end of the first part of her homecoming ritual. She touched him gently: his forehead, his hand, his chest.

He laughed and said exactly what her mother had: "You really shouldn't do that, Henriette!" Again she gazed at her fingers, still warm from the brief contact, laughed, and ran out into the garden.

The façade of their house, like those of their immediate neighbors, looked directly onto the street. The gardens of all three went back as far as the walls of the Castle—long rectangular plots separated by wooden fences higher than most people (including the Major, who was taller and lankier than anyone) could see over. The Helds' teemed with roses, nothing but roses, with large glass balls glinting on poles between them. The Elekeses' grew carefully tended and heavily scented petunias, violets, and mother-of-the-evening. The Major's was mostly flowering bulbs, with long-established conifers standing guard around a little pond, at the center of which a bronze fish gasped openmouthed, as if suffocating for the lack of water flowing through it.

For Henriette "home" was effectively all three houses, and her visits always took in both of the neighbors. She knew that, properly speaking, she ought to go back out into the street and enter by the front door or not at all, but she also remembered those strict instructions not to use that route, only the one behind the hedge at the bottom of the gardens. She knew that at the far end, behind the bushes, there was a place where the nails had been removed from some planks in each of the fences that separated their house from the others. The planks would move at a mere touch to create an opening, almost as if someone were waiting on the other side to receive her.

First she would push aside the boards at the bottom of the Birós' garden and slip through. There, Bálint was always waiting for her. She never, on these occasions, had to tell him how strange it was for her to see him looking so surreal, so very old, with his prematurely rounded back, and so thin—that troubling thought never occurred to her because, although the Bálint she was familiar with in her present life was almost fifty, on these trips home it was always the real one standing there, the one aged twenty-two. He accompanied her in silence as she carried out her round of inspection.

In the garden, nothing ever changed. The bronze fish still glinted in the sun, the water flashed, the fir trees stood darkly to attention, more black than green. Bálint never seemed surprised that she should want to take it all in. The governess, Mrs. Temes, was also aware of this habit, and even the Major had grown accustomed to it.

The moment she stepped inside and into the entrance hall she was struck by the characteristic smells of leather, turpentine, and mothballs. Seeing Mrs. Temes standing at the foot of the stairs, nodding and laughing, filled her with a longing to see the Major himself—the Major, that is, who used to live here, as he had been. That Major controlled everything around him with a glance, and Mrs. Temes would tremble in fear and wring her hands if she burned anything. But in his transformed state his behavior was unbearable. The moment he caught sight of his parents he would throw himself to the ground and become a child, cursing and blaspheming; his hands shrank to the size of a child's fist, smaller even than Henriette's, and he would shake them in fury at his father for forcing him to become a soldier. But here it was always the real Major, even when she found him dozing on the leather sofa, rigid in his slumbers, so unlike a civilian. "Only a soldier could sleep like that," she thought. She gently touched him too—face, lips, eyes, and eyelids, all warm to the fingertips.

Bálint followed her patiently everywhere while she carried out her tour of the house. In the dining room she found the nine chairs all present and correct, with the same pictures embroidered on their backs of young women carrying baskets from which spilled huge bunches of grapes. Mrs. Temes was the only woman in the house because the Major's wife had died soon after Henriette moved into the street. Whenever she went into the wife's room, Henriette always hesitated a moment, looked at Bálint, wondered whether to say something to him, and decided not to. He would never understand.

She passed straight through the salon. It was not a room she liked. No guests were ever entertained there, the windows were never opened, and the air was stale. She dwelt rather longer in Bálint's room, among the sheet music and the medical textbooks. One of its walls, the narrowest, was almost entirely taken up by a portrait of the Major's late wife, shown as a slim, smiling young woman standing on a patch of grass before an unnaturally large expanse of sky, with the child Bálint on her knee, snuggled up against her.

On the landing where the wooden staircase turned she found the bowl of fruit that was always left there for her when she came back, and greedily ate the handful of cherries. Then, assured at last that nothing here had changed, she breathed a sigh of happiness and continued on her way to the Elekes house. She went back the way she had come. Mrs. Temes watched her, shaking her head in disapproval: it wasn't right to go come and go by way of the fence. But she said nothing. It was what the Major wished, and the Major always knew best. Bálint went with the girl. It was part of the order of things that he should accompany her, and then wait for her in her own garden until she had finished her inspection of the Elekes house and returned, bringing Irén and Blanka with her. Running to the gap in the fence between the houses she once again caught the unvarying hum of her father's drill.

Here the opening was much larger, ten times the size of the first. At the mere touch of her little finger half of it slid down and there stood the Elekeses' house and garden. On the other side of the fence Blanka was waiting for her, and she was immediately assailed by the almost brutal scent of the flowers. Blanka was in tears, but that was no surprise: Blanka was always in tears; something was always happening to upset her. Now she followed Henriette just as Bálint had done in the previous garden, floundering along behind her in her clumsy wooden clogs. Henriette was all too familiar with the unreal Blanka—she had spent quite enough time with her on that clifftop, with the sea churning and foaming below—but she had no desire at this moment to think of the island where that version of her friend now lived.

The two girls went first into the study. There Uncle Elekes was in his usual place in front of the bookshelves, correcting children's homework beneath the bust of Cicero, the skin on top of his marble-like head gleaming softly. He didn't look up. Henriette was always delighted when she found him writing or reading, absorbed in words on a page. In the morning room she found Auntie Elekes, sewing her cushions as usual—Lord knows how many!—with scissors and reels of cotton spread all around her and her thimble lying abandoned. There was another Auntie Elekes, one who took the unreal Uncle Elekes out for walks and was thin as a wisp of thread herself, but this was the real one, the cushion-maker, plump as one of her own creations. The chaos in the room was appalling, with every seat and chair buried out of sight under random odds and ends.

Irén she would always find in the dining room, laying the table. With her, putting out even the most commonplace spread of snacks took on the quality of a ritual, as for an important birthday celebration. She never looked at Henriette or even greeted her. Until they had gone together back to the Helds' neither of them would greet the other or speak. Irén was wearing an apron, and not a hair on her head was out of place, even though she was leaning over her work. She was the only one whose unreal form was anything like her real one, even at this age. At forty-four she still came hurrying home with the same rapid steps, the same immaculate hair. The university lecture notes on her desk in the girls' shared bedroom were stacked neatly together. Beside Blanka's bed lay scattered piles of schoolbooks and an upturned inkwell. Everything in the kitchen, the entrance hall, and the bedroom was exactly as it had been. Reassured that nothing had changed, Henriette felt that life could begin again.

Irén and Blanka followed her through the gap in the fence, as Bálint had done earlier. He would always be standing exactly where he had left her. Again, nothing was said, not even an exchange of greetings, but everyone knew what Henriette wanted. The three girls took up positions at the corners of a triangle, with Bálint in the center as dictated by the rules of the game. "*The cherry tree leans over / Casting a long dark shadow / Where the dark little girl / Sits below...*" The circle they made around him by stretching out their arms was a tight one, difficult to turn inside. "*She is the one I love, / She is the one I choose.*" Only Henriette and Blanka sang, Henriette's voice soft and faint, Blanka's strong and firm. The humming of the drill accompanied the song but did not drown it out. "*Take her now, dear heart, / Take up the one you love, / Whirl her away . . .*" Bálint reached out and drew Henriette to him. The two other girls were not enough to sustain the circle, and their arms fell. They stood watching Bálint and Henriette spinning around together—Irén in silence, Blanka continuing to sing. The sun always shone when Blanka was at home.

MOMENTS AND EPISODES

1934

HENRIETTE always insisted that she had a perfectly clear memory of the day they moved into Katalin Street, but that could hardly have been true. If by "remember" she meant things she could recall directly herself, then that extended only to the general upheaval and excitement, the train going over the bridges, and the faces of one or two people who would play important roles later on in her life. Everything else had been told her by her parents, by the Elekes family, or by Bálint, who was the oldest of the four children and the one with the clearest recollection of events. Likewise, with the exception of a single sentence, her "recollection" of what had been said on that day had also come down to her, in all its detail, through her parents or the other children. She had, after all, been just six years old when they moved from the country.

The excitement of moving and the general disarray that led up to it had stayed with her because it was all so unlike what usually prevailed in their house. The fact that she was leaving her grandparents behind—grandparents with whom she had had such frequent contact—did not really register with her. She could see that it was something that gave her parents real concern, and she heard them promising each other that they would visit the old people regularly and have them to stay, but she had no idea what separation really meant. Nor did the idea of moving to Budapest mean much to her. She had been born there, but she knew very little about it.

Henriette had always been a rather solemn child, but it surprised her parents to see quite how upset she became once the move began. They themselves had both been rather happy as children and they thought that young people always rather enjoyed it when their home was turned upside down. But when the men started taking their belongings out, Henriette stood watching them, helpless, disconsolate, and increasingly distressed, and her mother had to stop what she was doing and sit with her, pressing the mutely protesting little body to her side. One after another the larger items of furniture were uprooted from their familiar places, left standing for a few minutes by the front door, then hoisted swiftly into the van; or they appeared one by one from all directions, made their way through the clutter in the room, out into the street, and up to the top of the stack already on board. Meanwhile, in the middle of every room, huge trunks and plump wickerwork baskets filled to overflowing with smaller items stood waiting their turn. Henriette knew that they were going away and would have to take all their possessions with them, but seeing it happen horrified her. Her father had too many other things to deal with to be able to spend time with her, so the task of coping with this unexpected reaction fell to her mother. Mrs. Held was filled with concern about what sort of life there might be in Pest for a child who was so comfortably settled where she was, who really loved her home, her friends in the street, and the whole neighborhood: a child, in short, who was so happy in that town. But her fears proved groundless. Henriette quickly stopped thinking about her old home, and when, as a much older child, she saw images of it in a film, she could identify the principal buildings and prominent statues only by her parents' animated response.

Once their possessions had gone, her mother traveled on ahead, leaving her to spend a few days with her father in a local hotel. The separation from her mother had also faded from her memory, no doubt because she rarely spent as much time with her father as she did with her mother, and when she did, the joy of being with him cast a radiance, even a sense of being "at home," over the strangeness of the hotel and the dining room where they ate.

They told her that she had enjoyed the train journey, and she could well imagine that. Train journeys always begin with little presents, the sort of trifles sold only in stations, and on this occasion her father had made her drop some money into the side of a machine shaped like an iron hen and pull out a drawer containing a metal egg filled with sweets. Her toys at home were all of the well-made, improving variety, so this frivolous and grotesque piece of commercial flummery came as a thrilling novelty.

What she did remember was crossing the bridges. The first time they went over one, on the way to Budapest, she was terrified. It was the first long journey she had ever made, the first time she had traveled over a river, and she lived the experience with all the intensity of childhood: to be traveling over water, in a train! She had first seen the river in the distance, then suddenly they were roaring across the bridge, clattering and banging between iron girders that kept racing toward them. She screamed and began to sob. It wasn't that she was afraid of the water. She wasn't thinking that the bridge might collapse. It was the noise that terrified her, this sudden clattering and banging that had not been there before they reached the bridge and then stopped the moment they left it.

Before they reached the next one her father made her lie down on the seat and covered her ears with his hands. That shut out most of the uproar, but the rest of her little face peered out between his palms in terror, and the tears kept coming. When they got to Pest and had to cross over the Danube to reach the Watertown district and their new home, he blocked her ears once again as a precaution. But this time their carriage ran much more quietly.

Henriette was reminded of this last detail some years later, when she was much older. She ran straight to the mirror to see what she looked like with her ears covered and immediately pulled her hands away. There was something grotesque, terrifying even, in what she had seen. "How horrible," she thought. "A face with its ears torn off by fear."

How and where she first heard mention of the Biró family was beyond her recall, but she had always thought of the name as having a special significance. Probably her father had talked about them when the idea of moving to Pest was first mooted. The term "Great War" meant nothing to her at the time, though she did know that her father had been in the army. It was only much later that she came to understand his relationship with the Major. At this stage she knew only that a good friend of her father's would be a neighbor, and how delightful it was that they had been able to buy the house next door to him. It took several more years for her to piece the details together.

Immediately on graduating Mr. Held had volunteered for the front, where his exceptional aptitude and courage brought him to the Major's attention. Until the 1940s none of this, or the various honors he had won, had meant much to Henriette. Only in time did she realize that his gold medal for bravery had become a symbol, a steel bolt in the fabric of their existence, a thing on which their lives and safety depended. Once that bolt was removed, everything else would come crashing down.

Her father's friendship with the Major had been kept up after the war, and when they decided to move to the capital, he had found the house for them and told them who their other neighbors would be, adding how pleased he was that they would be living in such close proximity. The Elekes family had never been talked about much in Henriette's old home because her father knew very little about them, only what the Major had told him.

Again, none of this was what Henriette remembered, only what she was told later. But she did recall the car turning into Katalin Street. She had seen the church and the statue in front of it—a woman standing on a wheel—and there was a narrow little street with houses on one side but no buildings along the other, only an avenue of short lime trees with thick trunks and the Danube glittering between them. The houses—tall, narrow edifices standing at the foot of Castle Hill—were very different from the ones she was used to. Of the Castle itself she knew nothing. It was a source of awe and wonder, like an illustration from her book of fairy tales. At the far end of the street was a strange little construction whose nature and purpose she could not begin to imagine. Where she had lived before she had never seen a European-style well, let alone a Turkish one. It must have been early summer, because there were blossoms on the lime trees and she had noticed the scent.

At the door of her new home she found her mother waiting for her, with Margaret at her side. Her father let go of her hand and she ran to Mrs. Held. She was so overcome with joy that she didn't tell her about the bridge crossings, though the experience was still very much with her. The sheer wonder of having a home again, even more beautiful and spacious than the old one, with Margaret there too, and being close to her mother again, thrilled her beyond words. There her memories faded and wandered elsewhere within that first day. Now her mother was standing in the arched entrance hall, not with Margaret this time but with a woman she did not know. This in itself was no surprise. Strangers were always coming and going at the Helds'. What was surprising was the woman's slatternly appearance. Instinctively tidy herself, Henriette could only stare at the sagging folds in the stockings and at the dress, which was not very clean and seemed to have been thrown on in a hurry. What astonished her even more was that when she went back into the house two girls came out of her bedroom—her bedroom! One was dark-haired, the other fair. They stood in the doorway, looking much more at home than she did—she whose actual home it was—each clutching one of her toys. Their faces and what they were wearing were printed on her memory in every detail. "These are your new friends!" her mother announced. Henriette just stood, staring at these "friends" of whose existence she had been so completely unaware. But the fact of their existence, and their obvious acceptance of her, filled her with comfort and contentment.

Both were older than she was. The taller one was dark-haired, a quiet, slow-moving, gracious girl; the younger seemed altogether more vivacious and bore a striking resemblance to the woman in the wrinkled stockings. The house, which had all this time been spinning dizzily around her under the torrent of new impressions, came suddenly to rest, supported now, as on two caryatids, on the shoulders of these two girls, the dark one and the fair. The former seemed almost as solemn a person as Henriette herself. The fair-haired one was in constant movement, wriggling like an eel. Never in her life had Henriette seen anyone quite so restless.

Timidly, as if she, not they, were the visitor in the house, she shot a glance past the two girls into her room. The dark girl immediately stepped aside, put down the toy she was holding, took the second one from the fair-haired girl and set that down too. Henriette passed between them into the room, and they immediately followed. She picked up the metal egg she had been given at the station and started to shake it, making it rattle. She had not yet taken any of the contents out: she had neither opened it nor wanted to. That was the source of its magic—laid by an iron hen, who could say what else might be hidden inside? The younger girl snatched it out of her hand and immediately began taking it apart with her deft little fingers. Sweets of all colors tumbled out into her palm. She picked one up to eat it, but then, as if suddenly realizing that something was due to Henriette, pushed a piece into the newcomer's mouth and passed the egg to the darker girl. The dark girl refused the sweet. She pushed the two metal halves of the egg back together, returned it to Henriette, and sternly told the younger one, "It's hers."

They often retold this story as being so typical of all three girls, adding that the grown-ups, who had been watching them from the other room, had burst out laughing. They had been joined by a balding man with a mustache, the husband of the sloppily dressed woman. Mrs. Held immediately began to compliment the dark-haired girl—such a well brought up little person. The girl listened without altering the expression on her face, but the fair-haired one gave a bright smile, as if she were the one being praised. Mrs. Held then opened the egg again, spread the contents onto a plate, and gave it to Henriette to offer around. Henriette did not much like sugary things, or anything in fact that was very sweet. What she really liked about the egg was that it didn't have to be thought of simply as a source of nice things to eat. With the lump of acidic sweetness in her mouth that the fair-haired girl had forced on her, she began doing the rounds with the plate. Her mother had not told her who to offer them to, so she thought that the adults should be included. No sooner had she begun when the doorbell rang. Margaret went to open it, and a man came in: a man in uniform. With him were an elegant, red-haired woman and a boy, visibly older than the other children. Borne along by her mother's instruction, Henriette offered the sweets to them too.

By now the room was full of people, and everyone seemed to know everyone else. Mr. Held and the uniformed man embraced. The smartly dressed woman with the red hair was called Mrs. Temes. Neither this first meeting nor the moment when she had offered them sweets were actual memories: they too were things she had been told about. What she did recall directly was that the boy and the two girls suddenly disappeared, almost before her eyes, through some exit that she was still unaware of, not yet having had the chance to explore the house. Margaret put out some brandy glasses on the sideboard, and the adults sat down to chat. Henriette remained standing, but no one paid her any attention. After a while Margaret took her outside, told her to go and play with the other children, who would certainly be expecting her, and showed her the way into the garden. That was her first sight of it, teeming with roses.

The three children, the dark girl, the fair-haired one, and the boy, were standing motionless in the center, between the beds of flowers, as if waiting for something to happen. She knew at once that it wasn't her that they were waiting for, but as she made her way timidly toward them she sensed they might at least be prepared to accept her. The fair-haired girl took her by the arm and gave it a tug, not unkindly but in friendship. The dark-haired one asked her what she was called, and how old she was, and Henriette introduced herself.

"I'm Irén," the dark-haired girl replied. The little fair-haired one said nothing but just smiled. Eventually she said she didn't have a name. Henriette believed her, though she thought it very strange.

"She's called Blanka," the boy said. "She's daft."

Henriette looked at her in trepidation. Blanka was spinning around and laughing as if she had just been paid a compliment. Then she pointed to the boy and sang out, "Bálint."

"All right, that's enough now," said the boy. "Shall we play or go back inside?"

Henriette stood beside the water tap and watched as they scattered like butterflies. They were playing a complicated form of tag. Henriette had never been able to run very fast: she was too unsure of herself, too clumsy. The little fair-haired girl was quick as the devil, and saucy with it. When the boy caught up with her, she tripped him and he fell, grazing his knee. He stood up and cuffed her firmly round the head, and she gave a loud scream. The dark-haired girl ran swiftly and gracefully: Henriette could only stand and watch, thinking that no one would ever catch her. What she was feeling all this time, she couldn't explain. Only much later would she manage to find words for it. But by then she was no longer alive.

The game came to an end as abruptly as it had begun. Everyone stopped in full flight, as when a sudden thought strikes the mind. The boy was the first to stop, and, having no one to chase, the girls halted in their turn.

"She must play too," he declared, looking at Henriette. "It's their garden."

"We can go back to ours," said the fair-haired girl. The dark-haired one stayed silent.

"No," said the boy. "We aren't going anywhere. Our parents are here. Henriette will play with us. Don't you have another name? Henriette is a terrible name."

Mortified, she whispered her denial. That moment stayed with her too, that feeling of utter shame. She would experience it once again, in the distant future, but in reverse: everything eventually comes round again, the living experience and the old memory sitting neatly side by side, just as a glass placed against a mirror behaves like a mirror. The name she was known by on that later occasion was Mária Kis.

"All right. Never mind. Come and join in."

She did. She got caught every time. Soon she was so upset she burst into tears. The boy stopped in mid-chase and stood deep in thought. The dark-haired girl studied her with the polite bemusement of a doctor attending to a patient he feels he can no longer help. Seeking to comfort her, the little one surprised her by putting an arm around her neck, but the arm was sweaty and rough, the contact painful, and the attempt was not a success.

"We should play something she can manage," the boy said. "She's only little and not very sporty."

"The Cherry Tree?" asked the fair-haired girl.

"The stupid Cherry Tree?"

This game was one she didn't know, so they taught it to her. She loved it. She picked up the tune at once, and though her voice was very soft she sang it perfectly. The fair-haired girl sang loudly and with gusto; the dark-haired one and the boy stayed silent. Round and round they went, for as long as they could keep it up. Whenever she was in the middle she chose Bálint, but he always chose the girl with the dark hair.

Suddenly they became aware that they were not alone. As in the final scene at the opera when all the dramatis personae are brought together onstage, everyone was there, standing at the gate—the man in uniform, the smartly dressed woman with red hair, Henriette's father, the slovenly woman, the bald man with spectacles, and Mrs. Held. Mrs. Held came toward them, then suddenly stopped, leaned over to inhale the scent of a crimson rose, and declared, "We shall live here till the day we die."

That was the one sentence spoken on that day that had stayed in Henriette's memory. She had no idea what it meant. She had no idea what life was, or death.

So what do you really know about us? Or about her? *Her?* Nothing.

What you do know is fragmentary and superficial, and even where it is true things aren't quite as you imagine them to be. The witnesses, the people who could say what really happened, are all either dead or keep their silence. Bálint, for example, knows the truth, but he doesn't talk about it, either to you or to me. Blanka also knows: she knows everything, apart from one particular detail. But she is farther away now than the stars, and Mr. and Mrs. Held, Henriette, and the Major are all dead. Drifting on a current of her own making, Mrs. Temes floats in a sea of forgetting, her huge cakes and pastries bobbing on the rolling waves before her, because she never gets enough sweetness in the old people's home. Mrs. Temes no longer knows who she is, never mind who the rest of us are now.

But she must have seen as much as any of us, and she wasn't stupid. She obviously worked out what she didn't know directly and drew her own conclusions; either that, or she simply asked Bálint. She would have had no difficulty in forming an opinion of the people in our house, even when she no longer lived among us—and not just because we were neighbors but because we were so easy to characterize, or at least appeared to be: my mother so beautiful and so stunningly

untidy; my father so earnest, a real stickler; Blanka so way-
ward and impetuous; and I so orderly and so perfectly well-
behaved.

"Irén, you never cause me a moment's concern!" she once
said to me when I stopped her at the front door and showed
her my school report. I just stared at her. I never felt I received
enough recognition, let alone praise. I stood there waiting
for her to say something nice about me, or to stroke my arm.
I couldn't imagine that there might be anyone on earth who
could get by without other people's care and concern.

So why did she not add, "But I do worry about your father,
I worry about your mother, and I am really concerned about
your sister"? She must have heard my mother's shrieks and
screams coming through the fence, the shrill protests and
complaints when she and my father had their rows, and my
father's attempts to reason with her and calm her down. I
once asked them why they had married. I was desperately
embarrassed, but every bit as polite and respectful as I always
was when I addressed them. Young as I was, I did realize
how improper it was to ask one's parents such a thing. I have
no idea what sort of answer I was expecting. I was looking
for an explanation as to how such utterly different people
could have come together and managed to produce two
children from their union. I was completely taken aback
when they replied, in chorus, "Because we loved each other."
Love, that blind, unreasoning force that drives people into
one another's arms and entangles their lives together, had
never seemed as believable to me in books as it was in their
marriage, their unswerving loyalty to one another, and when
I learned later on about the sly little god of antiquity who
shoots an arrow through the hearts of incompatible mortals
and wings his way laughing into the distance, I found him

a very real figure. I lived with this couple, and I observed them. I registered their differences through sound—my mother's endless prattle, her chortling laughter and loud shrieks, and my father's slow, considered, beautifully phrased speech. But none of these differences, however revealing, made the least difference. Nor did the suffering they inflicted on one another, whether consciously or not. The sad couple were in love.

But even as a child it never ceased to astonish me how little either of them understood me. My hard work, my desire to get on, my strict sense of duty, and my self-discipline meant to them merely that I was a success, that I was perfect, the one child they could hold up as their achievement, both to the world and to themselves after one of their painful scenes: "See, everyone, this is Irén, who combines the very best of her parents—hardworking and punctilious like her father, promising to become every bit as attractive as her mother, without the social awkwardness of the one or the fecklessness of the other!" My achievements, my praiseworthy efforts, my unremitting application were taken simply as evidence that I wanted to please them, to make their difficult lives a little easier. Sitting at the supper table, I would look on in constant amazement at Blanka's regularly tear-strewn face (because the evening was the only time my father had for administering the daily discipline); at my mother, in a grubby housedress just a shade too frivolous for the wife of a headmaster; at my father, in his meticulously correct suit, fixing everyone with his eye from behind his plate as if from behind his desk. Did it never occur to them that it was for myself that I wanted to succeed, without the least consideration for whether it made them happy or not?

If, for some psychologically obscure reason, they had taken

up the ridiculous notion that it would make them happy if I stopped studying or became a wastrel, I would have carried on working just as hard as ever, because I was preparing myself for adulthood and independence, as for a particular career. I was determined that one day I would live according to my own inclinations. And even as a young girl I knew what those inclinations would be. I wasn't looking for a perpetual funfair, a life of idleness in a heaven-size sweetshop. I wanted Bálint. Bálint and the Biró house, and the silence that seemed to envelope him when he played with us, even when he had to shout things out as part of the game—that inner silence for which, as a child, I had no name but for which I deeply longed. If I was good, and clever, and studied hard, and if my behavior was always beyond reproach, then obviously the Major would be delighted when his son chose to marry me, and I would make the perfect wife for Bálint, who was to become a great doctor when he grew up. And of course, if everyone was always so pleased with me, then perhaps the Major and Mrs. Temes might be prepared to overlook the fact that our house was constantly filled with quarreling, that my mother was as she was, and that Blanka was forever wailing and getting herself smacked. Being a child, I imagined that everyone who mattered to me would stay exactly as they were, would be there to see how well Bálint and I fitted in together, and would follow us on our passage through life the way Blanka and Henriette would walk behind us carrying the long train of my dress at our wedding (no doubt the nearest they would ever get to seeing one up close—no one would want to marry either of them, despite the Helds' belief that Henriette was the center of the universe and the fact that my mother loved Blanka so much more than she did me).

I had no difficulty noticing my mother's preference for Blanka. But when she lost her temper with her, there was something frenzied and indiscriminate about the way she pummeled her. It wasn't the way you would smack a child to discipline her; it was more like an attack on another adult, a sister rather than a daughter. But I was never jealous of Blanka. I had adored her from the moment she was first lifted up for me to see, and my mind dwelt constantly on the once unimaginable idea of having a sister born. She was an ideal companion. My father went through torments to make her learn her lessons and reach the minimum grades to pass in all her subjects, and the contrast made me stand out all the more for my application and industry. I was the role model held out to her time after time. And yet when she looked at me, her eyes shone with that inexplicable expression of fidelity and joy that only dogs are capable of, when their eyes light on the person they acknowledge as mistress but who never pays them enough attention. My father was immensely proud of me, and so too was my mother—though in her case the feeling was qualified by the fear that the girl who was being so strictly brought up might one day apply some of the same discipline to her. But no one was ever as proud of me as Blanka.

My father was a wonderful teacher. In all my experience of schools, whether as a pupil or as a member of the staff, I never met a teacher as passionate as he was. If ever there was a hero of the profession, it was he. He was a hundred times more authoritative than I was, and had far greater integrity. I was hardworking, irreproachable, well trained, and thorough, but I would have been much the same in any other walk of life. For my father, school wasn't a place of work, it was a temple; the source not of his daily bread but of the very breath of life. Whenever mundane reality contradicted the great truths to which he so passionately subscribed, or revealed his simple, naïve verities to be false—the rabbit is not by nature timid, the fox not always cunning—his would be a face of thunder. And it was only later, after I became a teacher myself, that I suddenly understood why he was so patient in his marriage. The pedagogue in him was always on the qui vive. It relished the challenge of trying to drive something of substance into my mother's trifling brain: for example, by encouraging her, the way you would a primary-school child, not just to screw her hair up in a bun but also to wash it from time to time, and not to go out in shoes that hadn't been polished.

But this isn't what I wanted to talk about: it was the commendation cards. At this stage Blanka and I still slept in our parents' bedroom; it was only later that we had a room of our own. One night I woke with a start and watched my father, in the glow cast by the little lamp on the bedside chest, as he made his way around the room, pulling out drawers. The chaos in my mother's drawers had to be seen to be believed—it was only Blanka and I who knew where anything was. We loved opening them. We always found something strange and unexpected, at whose purpose we could only guess. Knowing that my father hated it when she left things lying around, the moment she heard his footsteps approaching she simply threw whatever was there into the first drawer or onto the first shelf that came to hand—never back in its proper place. She then immediately forgot where she had put it, and when she needed it again of course she couldn't find it. So she emptied everything onto the floor and left us to wade through heaps of discarded clothing, often when they were just about to go out somewhere. My father would complain, admonish, and plead with her, while the two of us tiptoed around them like mice. If my mother could have reacted the way my father's pupils did, or even like Blanka on those occasions when she showed remorse and admitted that he was right, he would have instantly calmed down. But she couldn't bear his schoolmasterly attitude. She would laugh in his face and remind him that she was an adult. If he didn't like the way she ran the house, he should hire someone a bit more efficient than Rose. Look at the Major's house, where Mrs. Temes saw to everything, and what a wonderful help Margaret was to Mrs. Held! Or she would yell at him that his mania for order made him utterly impossible. This led to the scene where the characters murder each other, one of them screaming and waving her arms, the other arguing and protesting, while we, the silent chorus, stood by and watched.

Sooner or later one of us would find the missing article and they would be able to leave. From the way they walked off together, side by side, it was obvious that none of what had just happened was of the slightest importance. The storm had blown over. In fact, my father might have been rather less happy if he'd had his way. That would have left only Blanka to correct and admonish. He would have had nothing more serious or challenging to do than break the will of a child.

On that particular evening he was hunting for a button to go on his shirt. He had searched in every place he could think of, walking back and forth by the light of the bedside lamp. He knew there would be no point looking in the drawer of the worktable—there was only writing paper in there, and a little cup with a broken handle that was waiting to be mended. I sat up in bed and watched him, but he didn't notice me and carried on moving around the room. I couldn't see my mother's face, just her bare shoulders and her back. Even in sleep she was a figure of beauty and repose. I knew very little about sexual matters, but even at that age I sensed that they were able to give each other some deep happiness during the night that was far more intense and fundamental than the bitter squabbles of the day. Blanka was sound asleep, and I could see very little of her face.

I have no idea why, but at that moment I felt a love and pity for him that I had never felt before or have indeed since, even now that I know the difficult situation in which he lives and what it means to him to have lost his sight. Perhaps it was the night, and the silence, that helped me understand how deeply lonely he was, and how heavy the thoughts that weighed on his drooping head.

When he started rummaging again in the drawers that he had already been through, it broke my heart. I knew how hard he worked, how exhausted he must be. So at last I whispered, "It's in the kitchen, in the bowl on top of the kitchen scales." He put down the shirt he had been holding, looked at me, nodded once or twice, but said nothing, obviously not wanting to wake the others. There was no praise for the help I had given him. Instead he put his hands together and placed his head against them, telling me to go back to sleep. I didn't. I waited for him to come back. I was now afraid that Rose might have found the buttons lying around and moved them somewhere else, so he would have gone downstairs for nothing. But no, when he came back he was holding the little display card they were fixed on. He found a needle and thread, and started to sew.

Without saying a word I got out of bed, went over to him, and took the shirt and the needle out of his hand. He stood beside me and watched as I worked. I was still very small then, but very skillful and every bit as orderly, precise, and methodical as he was. The light from the bedside lamp cast shadows on the wall and they followed the tiny movements of my hand. All was silence, apart from the barely audible breathing of my mother and Blanka. He stood there as I worked. In my hand gleamed the immaculate shirt that had been put ready for the morning in the drawer—with a button missing halfway down the front.

When I had finished, he whispered his thanks and left the room. I went back to my bed and snuggled down, feeling suddenly very tired. It didn't surprise me that he had gone back to his study. He often stayed up late, writing articles for professional journals or poems for special occasions, and sometimes letters. What did surprise me was finding him standing beside my bed again. I looked up at him anxiously, a sick feeling in my stomach. Perhaps my work hadn't been up to standard? Every failure distressed me: I couldn't bear imperfection in the most trivial things. All thought of sleep had vanished.

There was a slip of paper in his hand. I had no idea what he wanted. Perhaps he wanted to give me a kiss and go to bed at last. But he made no move; he just stood there holding the paper. In the light of the bedside lamp it took on the same surreal gleam as the shirt. It occurred to me that perhaps, for some strange reason, he wanted me to see what he had written on it, to read the letter or whatever it was on the slip of paper. I reached out and his fingers let it fall on the bedcover. When I saw what it was the blood rushed to my face.

As the headmaster of the school we attended, he was the one who had introduced the practice of giving out gold and black cards of commendation or blame. We collected these

cards and handed them in at the end of the year. Our teachers then counted them up, and those who had the greatest
number of golds were given a special prize. At speech day
the winners were brought up onto the podium in the middle
of the school courtyard to stand beside my father and be
rewarded with a book. Parents could also ask for a gold or
black card for a pupil whose behavior at home had been either
exceptionally good or the reverse, and they regularly made
requests for the former, to acknowledge the domestic ac-
complishments of their daughters. In our house there was
certainly no shortage of opportunities to do this. Even as a
young child I regularly did more than enough, taking full
adult responsibility for my mother or for Blanka. But my
father was anxious to preserve his impartiality. He had often
asked for black cards for Blanka but never a gold one for me.

And now there was this letter in my hand, addressed to
my teacher:

Dear Sir,
My daughter Irén has sacrificed her sleep to perform
a task with special diligence and care. Please consider
her for a gold commendation.

Respectfully yours,
Abel Elekes, Parent

We looked at each other—he with that little half smile,
the one I so seldom saw, softening his craggy features, and
I, completely unsmiling, suddenly very upset and close to
tears. Every year since I had been at the school I had stood
beside him on the podium and he had shaken my hand. At
the end of every year I had listened to the applause and sa-
vored the sweet taste of success as he presented me with a

book. But that particular year my hopes had been dashed. I had missed a whole quarter due to scarlet fever and had struggled to make up what I had missed. My marks were all outstanding, but for three months I had been out of school and had no opportunity to gather cards. The letter brought with it all the pain of an old wound opening: that he should only now, for the very first time, be prepared to help me in this way, despite the fact that I had always been so attentive and good, and that I was forever tidying up after my mother and Blanka. He should have been asking for gold cards for me every day. Rose wasn't up to the job of keeping the house tidy, and if it weren't for me the place would have been in total chaos. Sometimes, when my father was in an even grimmer mood than usual and she was frightened by his silences, my mother would tell outright lies, claiming that it was Blanka, not she, who had done whatever it was. Blanka would take the blame, submit to the chastisement that followed, and be rewarded later with an apple, a piece of chocolate, or a ribbon for her hair. It was a game they played. I was the only one who was straightforward and honest.

"Are you happy?" he whispered, and once again that little half smile lit up his face. "You've been such a good girl tonight." I made no reply. He took that as a "yes," and switched off the light so that I wouldn't see him getting undressed. I was still awake when I heard his breathing become regular and I knew he had fallen asleep. My little Kinga has the same ability to nod off quickly and easily.

I was unhappy as only a child can be. The letter was still on the chair beside my bed, where I had laid out my carefully brushed clothes and fresh underwear for the morning. I fumbled around for the piece of paper and brushed it off onto the floor.

The next day I handed it in to my teacher. I was given a gold card in exchange and dropped it in the bag where I kept the others. Every student had the identical bag, made by their mothers according to a prescribed pattern: mine had been made by my father when I was still in a junior class. Blanka, who very occasionally, when she was bored, liked to imitate me, saw the bag in my hand and took out her own. She had five gold cards. Lord knows how she had come by them—she never collected that many in a whole year. Now I thought a bit more kindly toward my father than I had the night before: what torments he must have put himself through to get her—on five separate occasions—to the level where she could perform so well! Or perhaps he had finally managed to explain to her that she should pull herself together, and they were for exemplary conduct.

She laid her cards out in a pattern. She was thrilled with them, and counted them again and again, unable to believe that there should be so many. Anger and bitterness swept over me, and something happened that very rarely did between us—I shouted at her: why was she trying to annoy me, showing off with her crummy little cards? She knew absolutely nothing, her work was useless, and I wasn't going to be first in my class this year despite all my hard work just because I hadn't been able to collect all the cards I needed.

She made no reply—she was used to being scolded. She just picked her things up and took herself off. I saw little of her for the rest of the day. She went to the Helds and stayed there, even when we called over the fence for her to come home. My mother went to get her and slapped her bottom, and once again she cried. She was grumpy all that evening. Then, without any warning, she was bright and happy again.

She became her usual silly and boisterous self, and surprised me by sidling up to me and giving me a kiss. I pushed her arm away—I just couldn't bear to be near her that evening, however hard she tried to placate me. Deep inside I knew she was not to blame for my anger toward her. We had another squabble shortly afterwards. It was as if the devil had got into her. She kept trying to grab my school satchel, and that always made me nervous. Like my father, I always kept my belongings spotlessly clean and tidy, and I couldn't bear anyone fiddling about with them. I pulled her away from my bag, she took fright and screamed yet again, and our father demanded to know what was the matter with us and what was the explanation of all this noise.

Finally, all was quiet. My mother was standing in front of the mirror trying on a shawl. Her hair was piled up on top of her head and fixed with a large comb, and she was wondering how she would look as a flamenco dancer. Blanka gazed at her in rapture. I suspect my father and I were both somewhat embarrassed.

The next day we handed in our commendation cards. I had no expectation of the outcome: I knew I wouldn't come first. When, during the final lesson of the day, my name was finally called out, I was filled with delirious joy, rather like the drunkenness that adults experience. For a moment I thought they had taken pity on me. They must have said in the staff common room that it didn't matter how many gold cards Irén Elekes had collected she had always been at the top of her class, so let her do it again; she should be there without the cards. I went up to the teacher's chair, my ears ringing. "What a way to keep your things!" the teacher smiled. "Dear oh dear, Irén."

I stared at him, dumbfounded. He could see that I had

no idea what he meant, and he shook his head. He emptied the contents of the bag out in front of me and they immediately fell into two piles, as if arranged by invisible hands. One lot lay smooth and shining on the table, the other was grease-stained, smeared with chocolate and ink, and torn. Five moldy gold cards were jumbled up with my immaculate commendations. "You seem to have made a mistake and brought your sister's as well," the teacher added. "You must never mess about with these cards." And he swept them up together and returned them to me.

That year Klári Kálmán came first, as she had the most gold cards. The lesson dragged on: never in my life had one lasted so long. At break I was the first to leave. I went straight to Blanka's classroom. My little sister was standing in the corner, with her back to the door. She was being kept in, I was told by her classmates, as a punishment for misbehaving yet again: she had forgotten to bring her commendation cards.

I went up to her. She must have sensed that someone was close behind her because she turned round. When she saw who it was, she blushed and smiled. Nobody could smile the way Blanka did.

My father had brought me up to be self-disciplined, and even as a child it rarely happened that I lost my self-control. Some inner principle always told me what I could or couldn't do. But now, for the very first time, my rage completely overwhelmed me. I grabbed the cards, ripped them to shreds, and hurled them in her face, at her body, at her feet.

"Idiot!" I yelled. "What do you think my bag is? A dump for your toys? For you to hide your dirty rubbish in? Don't you think I've enough to cope with right now?"

She made no reply. She didn't lower her gaze. She looked

straight at me, the tears welling up in her eyes: a look of sorrow and reproach. I had to knot my fingers together to stop my hands shaking. I had suddenly realized what she had been hoping to achieve when she stuffed her own cards into my bag. Unobservant as ever, she hadn't noticed that the pupil's name and class and its specific purpose were all printed on each card and that there was simply no way that I could have won first prize with the help of her wretched little commendations.

We stood face-to-face. I had no idea what to say next. Her classmates were making a terrific din, and one of them ran out to find their teacher. I heard her shouting down the corridor that the older Elekes girl was yelling and using bad language.

Now I was the one who sensed that there was someone standing behind me. Blanka's eyes told me who it was. I didn't have to turn round. I already knew, but not what would come next.

"What happened?" my father asked. "What's going on here?"

"I cheated," Blanka replied. And without a second thought she turned her back to us and knelt down facing the corner, the way she did in church during mass. In our school, being made to kneel was the worst punishment of all. Father did not ask her to explain, nor did he ask me. He took me by the shoulder, forced me down to the floor among the torn-up commendation cards, and stood behind us for a few minutes. Then I heard him shut the door behind him. Never before, in all my life, had I had to be punished. I wept so hard in my shame that I could no longer see either the wall or Blanka. But I felt her there, because after a while she leaned over and kissed me.

THE GIRLS were being helped into their costumes by Mrs. Held, and Bálint by Mrs. Temes. The costumes were not exactly unfamiliar. The children had been rehearsing in them for several days now, and Bálint for one was perfectly capable of dressing himself, but their having to be helped was all part of the fun. Mr. Elekes paced anxiously from room to room, and although only Henriette had been nervous at the start, her agitation slowly infected the other actors too. As soon as they were in costume Mrs. Held brought out the rouge and the eyebrow pencil and began to apply it: Irén first, then Bálint. This could all be done in the one room. The boy hated having his mouth painted, and his first reaction was to wipe it straight off, which of course was forbidden, but the girls were entranced by the whole process.

A stage had been constructed in the salon on benches brought home from the school. Mrs. Elekes, Mr. Held, and the invited audience of Rose and Margaret were waiting for the performance to begin, along with the Major, in whose honor the event had been arranged. The Major watched Mr. Elekes indulgently as he dashed across the room from time to time, urging patience and silence on the assembled company as if he were still in the classroom. There was something rather touching about his never-ending attempts to impose

71

stability on the uncertainties of life, if only by marking and celebrating every special occasion. He had a thick, check-patterned notebook filled with speeches, poems, and plays commemorating the martyrs of Arad, noting days in the calendar dedicated to particular birds and trees, recording religious occasions and events within the family. Ever since the Helds had moved into the street everyone's name day and birthday had been honored in the special Elekes manner in each of the three houses.

Today it was the Major's turn. When the tradition was first introduced, the children had merely made little speeches, or one of them would play the piano or sing. Now that they were older Mr. Elekes considered them ready for greater tasks, and sometimes they performed entire little plays. On the previous occasion it had been Mr. Held's name day, and the play Mr. Elekes had written had been about the Good Dentist, with Henriette in a supporting role. She was the patient to whom the Good Dentist (Irén) brought relief, while the anxious parents (Blanka and Bálint), stood hand in hand and recited the eloquent poem that Mr. Elekes had composed in honor of the selfless healer. This time the Major, suspecting that a reference to his military connections would feature in the patriotic proceedings, had come prepared. He hated being a soldier and was ashamed that he had been forced to enter the profession, but he had long given up hope that Mr. Elekes would ever understand. The very first time he mentioned his feelings Mr. Elekes had given him a look of such horror—as if he had been told a dirty joke—that the Major quickly changed the subject. There could be little point in attacking his friend's fundamental beliefs over something he simply could not comprehend. Indeed, if Mr. Elekes's gentle heart were capable of such a base feeling, he might rather have envied his friend's gallant profession, that of protecting the lives of widows and orphans.

Others would soon forget the Major's thirty-fifth birthday celebration, but not Bálint. And even for him the picture was incomplete. It survived in separate segments, like an orange, that kept returning at random moments later throughout his life.

The celebration began with the ringing of a bell. The actors were ready at the back of the stage, standing behind a curtain Mrs. Temes had run up from an old sheet. First to step forward was Mr. Elekes himself, to deliver the birthday eulogy in person. It had the surprising effect of forcing the Major to lower his eyes in embarrassment. There was so much warmth and affection in the words, such an artless sincerity shining through them, that he could not fail to be touched. Hearing the speaker ask for God's blessing upon the Major and wishing that his guardian angel might never be far from his side, Margaret and Rose crossed themselves as if they were in church, and Mr. Held turned to him and shook his hand. Mrs. Elekes meanwhile was nervously chewing sweets: she could barely wait to see her children. Mrs. Held had already taken a seat beside her, and her eyes too were trained on the curtain. She had just come from Henriette, having seen how very much prettier and more touching she looked than the two other girls, and she felt that, even though they had failed to persuade her to take a speaking part, she would have only to be seen to outshine the others.

The children listened to the peroration from behind the curtain. The words passed mostly over their heads. "Glory," "manliness," and "honor" meant little to their ears, apart from Bálint, the oldest of them and the most capable of understanding such concepts. It made him feel how unthinkable it was that he should be forced to become a doctor when there was such glory in the life of a soldier, and he waited with mounting impatience for the play to begin so that, onstage at least, he might proclaim something he would never otherwise have the chance to express—what a joy it would be to hold a sword in his hand, and how willingly he would give his life for his country should the need ever arise.

Irén, wearing her royal crown, was surprisingly, almost shockingly beautiful. Her father had felt that if she were to represent Hungaria she should appear in something rather grander than mere folk costume and had dressed her as an angel, without wings, in a long white pleated dress. The belt around her waist was studded with brightly colored stones, and on her head was the crown of St. Stephen, which Mr. Elekes had made himself from cardboard, taking considerable pains to bedeck it with artificial pearls and colored paper. Henriette, her page, stood throughout the prologue with her eyes fixed on the curtain. Even though she knew she would have nothing more to do than kneel at Irén's feet holding the national coat of arms, she found the prospect terrifying. Irén too was apprehensive. She had the major role, and Blanka, whose behavior on these occasions was always unpredictable, might well do something to put her off her lines. Blanka was the only one who was both aroused and amused by her situation, bowing merrily before her regal sister in her boy's costume. This was Blanka, with her dumpy little body, as she had been before she could even talk. Her soft curls, which Mrs. Held had attempted to tame with the application of a curling iron, had defied correction, and she fidgeted constantly while her father was speaking. Bálint had to grip her hand to stop her from hitting her father with her rifle while he was speaking on the other side of the curtain. When the applause died down Mr. Elekes returned to his place, and the Prologue metamorphosed into the Producer. He leapt onto the side of the stage and whipped the curtain back. It slid smoothly along the wire attached to the walls on either side with picture-hanging nails and wrapped itself around him as if he were Lazarus, a most patient Lazarus contentedly swaddled in his shroud.

The scene thus presented drew yet more applause from the onlookers. Irén was seated on a throne, her hands in her lap, the crown glittering against her dark hair; her gaze was fixed on the audience, her body perfectly, almost preternaturally still. At her feet knelt Henriette, pressing the national coat of arms rather too firmly against her knees. Mrs. Held's heart was torn by the sight, and her husband felt so sorry for the girl he quite forgot how much he had been looking forward to the children's play. Excellent teacher though he was, when it came to Henriette Mr. Elekes's instincts invariably let him down. Again and again he forced her to appear in front of audiences, but she had absolutely no self-confidence and any kind of public performance was a torment to her. Mr. Held squeezed his wife's hand, a gesture that betrayed how very much they both felt for their little girl in her fear, and how they would have liked to rush up to her on the stage and pluck her away back home. Every so often the heraldic shield wobbled in her hands, and the mountains and the river behind (represented by swathes of cloth) trembled in sympathy.

Looking at Irén-Hungaria, the Major found himself unexpectedly moved for the second time that day. His friend never explored new ideas, his pronouncements were never qualified, and if, on occasion, more was expressed in his plays than he intended, it was purely by chance, a random effect.

There on the makeshift stage sat Irén, the crown of the sainted king on her head, the trembling page at her feet. The page was white with fear, an orphan such as no orphan had ever been, and it was her presence that made it so harrowing. Hungaria herself looked unimaginably defenseless and alone. His eyes sought out the producer to try to determine from the look on his face whether he too had noticed the grim significance of the scene, but the schoolteacher was still covered by the collapsed curtain. There was only Mrs. Temes, the prompt, sitting with the script in her hand at the far corner of the stage.

Happily, the image of Hungaria sitting beneath her sacred crown with the little page trembling at her feet did not oppress him for long. From behind the curtain appeared Blanka, the child in a boy's costume, tiny rifle in her hand, a sturdy bag hanging at her waist, her plump little body straining against the tight trousers. She was in excellent form and, just this once, did not forget her lines.

She represented the Enemy, Hungaria's Enemy. She was nameless, from no particular country, the perennial foe come to attack the homeland, with a rifle trained on Hungaria. As a child Blanka had a penetrating voice—she had always enjoyed it when she was allowed to shout—and the adults giggled at her vigorous, well-articulated delivery. This did not please Mr. Elekes. He had intended the scene, and in fact the entire play, to be deadly serious.

Blanka began to heap insults on Hungaria. She accused her of every kind of base behavior, announced she would deprive her of her shield and crown, and threatened the page with her gun. The brief moment of good humor produced by Blanka's unexpected appearance vanished, and for the second time Mr. Held's heart skipped a beat: Henriette's lips were white with fear. It was clear that even in a play she could not bear to be threatened.

Then, with great dignity, Irén stood up to deliver her lines. She spoke beautifully, refuting in verse every allegation raised by the foe. In terms charged with far-reaching significance, she begged for help to defend her shield and her crown, crying out to every corner of the compass the one word, "Help!" Once again, the Major felt that he could no longer bear to look on and see his country presented thus onstage: it was a truly horrifying play. Her father-producer had dressed Irén as an angel, but her feet had been left bare to allow her to turn in supplication in every direction. Mrs. Temes lowered her exercise book: clearly the girl needed no prompting. Mrs. Elekes, entranced by her daughter's performance—and not actually listening to what either she or Blanka were saying—went on munching her sweets and basking in her children's cleverness. Tense as ever, Mrs. Held kept her eyes on her own daughter and ignored Irén. Finally, Bálint appeared.

The audience thought they had never seen such a handsome boy as he, dressed in his Hussar's uniform, and never had a sword been drawn with such grace. His part was also in verse, and he too spoke his words well, words of comfort for Hungaria: she had nothing to fear; he would fight for her; she need not fear for her shield, her crown, or her future. He was at her side. If necessary, he would lay down his life for her.

From behind the curtain Mr. Elekes saw Irén smile as she turned to face Bálint. It rather shocked him: she was supposed to look at him with devout fervor. It was only when the girl realized that Bálint had neither seen her smile nor taken the least notice of it—and hadn't returned it—that her expression became serious again. Bálint went on with his script, knowing that everything in it was true. Mr. Elekes's distinctive verse style exactly expressed his newfound sentiments—his readiness to die heroically, and the conviction that he, and only he, could save the country.

Irén, however, saw not Bálint the Hussar but Bálint the young man, and she hoped that he had noticed how very pretty she looked that day, how very grown-up in her full-length dress. Bálint was seeing something rather different. Standing before him in her long white robes and jewel-encrusted belt was not Irén Elekes but the embodiment of his country. He finished the speech, then fell to his knees, as instructed, and laid his sword at her feet. This brought his face close up beside Henriette's, and he saw her open her mouth as if she too wanted to cry out for help, or at least catch her breath. Bálint was very fond of Henriette, but this gasping for air like the fish in their garden pond filled him with a strong desire to smack her. Then he raised his eyes and gazed up at Irén.

For the first time he realized who she was. All thoughts of his father's birthday and the family play vanished, along with his lines. Beneath the sacred crown and the Hussar's busby their eyes met, to the exclusion of everything else. Bálint had no way of knowing that she felt the same physical reaction that he did, or that what he experienced at this moment was indeed physical. These were the first moments in their lives that he, with the sword in his hand, and she, with the sacred crown on her head, had any premonition of the thing that would later drive the two of them remorselessly together. All he felt in that instant was how wonderful it would be for the play to stop, to speak no more lines, and to remain just where he was, by her side.

He had no choice but to carry on. Blanka was at her most entertaining that afternoon and now she raised her rifle and began hurling abuse at him. Bálint grabbed his sword, leapt to his feet, and tried to wrestle the gun from her hand before she could take aim at either Irén or himself. At this point, according to the script, she was supposed to hand the weapon over, but she didn't. Instead her face became white and contorted with rage. Mr. Elekes and Mrs. Temes hissed furious instructions at her, to no avail. Bálint, following an adult instinct for the first time in his life, hurled himself at her and, being so much stronger than she was, managed to tear the weapon from her hand, whereupon her rage turned into a loud howling. Mr. Elekes was still struggling to disentangle himself from the curtain so that he could bring his daughter to her senses and get her to surrender to Bálint, then lie down dead at his feet for him to plant his boot in triumph on her chest and raise his sword towards Irén, to signal to the guest of honor that the finest soldier in the world was a Hungarian. It didn't happen, at least not in the way they anticipated. Without a word or even a sigh, Henriette keeled over, overcome by stage fright.

The performance came to a halt. Her mother's embrace soon restored Henriette to herself, but the play was over. Still in her costume, Blanka got a thoroughly good smacking from her mother. Only Bálint and Irén were left on the stage. Irén took off her crown, Mrs. Temes drew the curtain, and the two of them stood there, shut away from the other two, the sinner and her victim. Once again Bálint felt that disturbing and shameful impulse for which he had no name. He blushed bright red and fled from the scene.

Memories of this little play returned to trouble him three times in his later life. The third and last was in 1952, when they began to question him at the start of his disciplinary hearing. Blanka was seated close by, in a corner of the room.

Instead of attending to the questions, his mind, in something of a daze, somehow dredged up the lines Blanka had spoken that day. After a long pause, and to the amazement of the party official present, he returned not the sort of answer that was expected but a line of verse: "I shall attack you, I shall vanquish you, I shall chop your arms and legs to pieces."

The first occasion when it came back to him was ten years after it had taken place, on the day Henriette died. On his return from the hospital that night a tearful Mrs. Temes had led him outside to a chair she had placed beside the fence, so that he could use it to look over. Standing on it he saw the girl lying on the gravel path in the moonlight. Her neck was twisted to one side, just as it had been in that moment in their childhood when she had keeled over at Irén's feet.

The memory returned again shortly afterward, when he was taken prisoner during the siege of Budapest. As the line of captives moved off he suddenly thought of Irén. By then she was his fiancée, though she had no idea what was happening to him, and the Irén that came to his mind was not the slim, serious-minded university student but a vision clad in a white dress with a waistband of gleaming stones and the crown of St. Stephen on her head. The Russian guard had no idea what was passing through his mind when he suddenly came to a halt and stood there, his face buried in his hands, until they prodded him to keep moving. The guard could not have known that in his mind's eye Bálint was seeing himself in that scarlet Hussar's costume, with his little sword, the busby on his head, and also the Major, who was now dead, and the Helds, who had been taken away, and Henriette, who had been killed. He was trying to think where the Arrow Cross fanatics might have taken the crown of St. Stephen.

1944

I HAVE always been an early riser, but on that particular day I was up even earlier than usual.

Blanka had the blanket pulled over her head and didn't notice as I crept past her. I stood at the window and looked at our garden in the morning light. That year almost all the flowers we had planted happened to be red and the garden was ablaze with them. They made the golden light of the sun seem almost green.

I had been in love with Bálint for so long, and so ardently, that on this morning of our engagement my feelings were of two distinct kinds—not just how passionately, almost oppressively happy I was but that what was to happen seemed the most natural thing in the world, almost preordained. For what other conclusion could there have been to a love that reached back to our innocent childhood? It seemed to me that the flowers opening and flooding the garden with their scent, the rain having suddenly stopped the night before after persisting on and off for so long, and the sun shining in my face all existed because today was my day. From the window I went across to the mirror. I saw my face looking as radiant as the sun that shone on the garden on this special morning. I was beautiful, I was young, and I was happy....

That moment was again in my mind, years later, when Bálint and I stood in the registry office contemplating each other. We were smoking, and I was thinking how our hands in particular betray the passage of time, and how large and ugly mine had become. We had invited the two witnesses, Timár and my head teacher, to an Italian restaurant, and as we took our places, man and wife for the very first time, Bálint suddenly started to guffaw. At the same time, he was choking and gasping for breath, and our two friends stared at him in surprise. Timár topped up his glass and urged him to drink, his manner implying that this was a man who had gone through a very great deal and had obviously not yet come to the end of it. The head teacher shot me a worried glance—he clearly didn't think that kind of laughter was appropriate at a wedding—then he dropped his gaze. At this point a sense of the ridiculous welled up inside me too, and Bálint and I sat there, at opposite ends of the table, looking at each other and roaring with laughter. I have no idea what the weather was like. I seem to remember it was nice.

By this time Rose was no longer with us, to my considerable dismay. I had really loved her, and my disappointment at losing her was heartfelt. She had looked after Blanka and me since birth and had helped us all in a great many ways. Our mother had been completely casual about our diapers: either they were forever falling off or she would simply forget to change us. When we cried she invariably assumed we had colic and plied us with chamomile tea. She would do that for us, but she didn't change our diapers.

I too was frightened when the bombing started but much less so than the grown-ups. It always amazed me how pathetically terrified they became. I had difficulty understanding what death might mean, least of all my own. But Rose was so terrified she did something that none of us had thought her capable of. She had been really happy living with us, she adored my mother and viewed her performances and her unpredictable changes of mood as so much merry entertainment. Her leaving us meant that we—that is to say, my father and I—had to do everything for ourselves, and later when he was conscripted into the army, it all fell to me.

Our mother, having sworn in complete sincerity that we could leave everything to her, proceeded either to do nothing at all or to do things in such a way that made even more work for me. We had to excuse Blanka from the household chores, as far as we could, because she was about to take the last of her school exams and needed to perform reasonably well. She was hoping for a job in the hospital where Bálint was in his first few months as a doctor, and she was in a complete panic, frantically cramming and declaring that whatever she learned one day she forgot the next. Frankly, I couldn't find it in my heart to ask her for help.

For our engagement the Major came back from the front on a three-day leave. He left his batman behind, so the preparations were carried out by Mrs. Temes. The Held family were represented only by Henriette: they had a great many problems at this time and these included not being allowed to employ servants.

On the eve of the event we worked late into the night. My scatterbrained mother was so excited by the fact that her daughter was about to get married that she stationed herself on guard duty, sitting on the sofa to watch and shout out suggestions every now and then, most of them completely impracticable—though I was just as happy listening to them as she was yelling them out. My dear father gave himself up to the role of father of the bride, contented, complacent, even a little moved, wandering off from time to time to check on Blanka, who was confined to our bedroom with her schoolbooks, or taking a moment to sit and rest beside my mother on the sofa. When everything was at last ready, he escorted Henriette to the door of her house: that had been the strict condition on which Uncle Held had allowed her to come. Night and the hours after dusk were especially dangerous for them, and while Mr. Held was still personally protected by his war-service medal, Henriette was never allowed out of the house on her own even by day.

I was once again standing at the window looking out into the garden. Now of course I understand the significance of that instant, though I had no sense of it at the time. We always realize too late the importance of drawing out the moment while you can, while it is still possible. I didn't. I didn't savor it or hold on to it. I was in too much of a hurry. I just wanted the time to pass, for us to get breakfast over, fly off to church, come back, and sit down to the celebratory meal. Out of consideration for Uncle Held it was to be at midday and not in the evening. I wanted everyone to be there, everyone I cared for: that day was to be the fulfillment of my destiny. There was only one date ahead of me that would be even more important, the day I became Bálint's wife. So let everything begin!

It began.

The people who were with me on that day were imprinted on my memory—some of them permanently, some for many years afterward—exactly as they were at the time, both as they arrived at the house and in the way they conducted themselves.

Blanka woke with a yawn. Then, suddenly remembering what day it was, she held out her arms to me. I went over to her and kissed her round, childish, beaming face. I knew I wasn't the only one who was in love with Bálint: at various times Blanka and Henriette had been as well. I didn't mind; I never thought of them as dangerous rivals. Bálint was the sort of person who inspired that response from others without in the least intending to. You simply had to love him.

The eyes that met mine were neither envious nor sad. Had Blanka been the one about to become Bálint's bride she could not have been happier. My thoughts often went back to that moment, just as they did to the sight of Mrs. Temes coming into the bedroom carrying a tray, a strong, laughing, ever-cheerful, and reassuring figure. The Mrs. Temes I know today is very different—tearful and timid, her face empty, watchful, or lit up with greed. I didn't know then that some people die long before their real death. Nor did I imagine that the last time you saw them might also be the last time they were truly alive.

As for my mother, this was probably the first time I saw her pull herself together. She was very nicely turned out. She had taken a proper bath and gone to agonizing lengths with her hair and her clothes. She approached me with the smile of a naughty little girl, a very small child who knew that, yes, she was always at fault but see how clean she was now, and how hard she was trying. At breakfast she paid close attention to the way she ate and drank, and said nothing that was either stupid or shocking. It was as if she were rehearsing for the lunch, hoping to avoid disappointing the Major or giving the impression that the Elekes girl wasn't good enough for the Biró boy.

My father shot her the occasional surprised glance: a proud, almost amorous look. His habitual dignified reserve had softened to something like cheerfulness, no doubt with the growing realization that everything might yet turn out well, that his daughter might have not just a successful life but a happy one. I think he lived in the constant expectation that one day a sign would come down from heaven, the expression of God's recognition of his honest and vigilant labors, and that on that day, the day of my engagement, he felt it had come.

If I retain an image of the Helds it is of them seen from the back. Only after I had opened the window did I realize that they had just that moment walked past our house. I caught a glimpse of Uncle Held's erect, slim body, his striking blond hair, and Auntie Held's neat little person. I leaned out with the intention of calling out to them to be sure to get back in time and not be late for the lunch but decided not to—I was in the middle of cleaning the house, I had a cloth in my hand and a scarf around my head, which didn't seem altogether right for a bride-to-be. Nowadays, no matter how hard I try, I cannot conjure up their faces: just those two figures walking slowly, arm in arm, toward the Katalin Street church, moving steadily away from our house. In my dreams I call out to them, but they keep on walking, until finally they disappear from sight.

Then Bálint and Henriette arrived, together.

Even today I don't understand why it was only then, and not much, much earlier, that I realized I was jealous of Henriette. Ever since she had moved into the street she had somehow belonged not just to all of us but especially to Bálint. That he had never smacked her as hard as he did either Blanka or me was not in itself surprising. She wasn't the sort of person you would ever want to hit, being so quiet and timid, and the smallest of us three. There was a certain pleasure in slapping Blanka, in pinching her leg or smacking her bottom, but it was never like that with Henriette. Bálint sometimes inflicted pain on me too, though never again after the play when he had been the Hussar. We couldn't find words for it, but thereafter if we pulled each other about or caused each other physical pain it just seemed so wrong or, to be more precise, so strangely satisfying. So we stopped, and we never again had a fight. A little later, when we knew we were in love, we both did all we could to avoid arousing the other.

But at that moment, with the two of them standing before me, and Henriette with that solemn little smile on her face, I suddenly understood that her being there irritated me deeply. It annoyed me that she was a person in trouble who had to be cared for, that Bálint was standing by her side like a guard and I couldn't utter a word of complaint because in these insane times we simply had to look after her. That they should have come together was perfectly logical. I had seen the Helds going off myself, and Henriette wasn't allowed out on the street alone, so Bálint had obviously called to collect her. But that was no comfort to me just then. I cannot decide how reasonable my reaction was, because I did love Henriette. If they hadn't arrived together on the day of my engagement, I would never have had those feelings. I would simply have felt, as I always did, that the poor Held family were in a terrible situation, and that I wanted to be kinder and behave better toward her, because no one, least of all Henriette, should be put in the position they were in. I did love her, but seeing her at that time, on that day, standing there with Bálint, somehow got to me. She should have waited until her parents returned and come over with them. Why couldn't she have the tact, on our day of betrothal, to let Bálint and me have just five minutes together before the guests arrived?

I realize now that she was afraid, and that Bálint also

feared for her safety. No matter now. It is not only facts that are irreversible; our past reactions and feelings are too. One can neither relive them nor alter them. Henriette gave me a kiss, whispered something in my ear, congratulatory, no doubt, and pressed her cheek against mine for what seemed ages. I held her in an embrace, but there was not the slightest warmth toward her in my heart, only this feeling of vexation and annoyance. Then she stepped to one side and dropped out of sight, just as my father and my mother had, and likewise Mrs. Temes, who had been rushing in and out of our house since early morning. At the time I failed to register the soft thud of a door closing behind me; but later that day, when for the tenth or hundredth time I tried to reconstruct the sequence of events, the sound of that door came back to me in a flash, along with the fleeting glimpse of a red dress. It was Blanka. She had shepherded everyone out of the room, so that I could at last be alone with Bálint.

Never again did I see him the way I saw him in those few moments, and never again have I felt those same feelings for him. I believe now that that was our real marriage, our true married life together, those few short minutes the two of us spent there, not touching or moving toward one another, simply gazing into one another's eyes, beyond the need for expression, gesture, or action, simply surrendering ourselves to the stern and painful laws that direct the course of youth and love.

That was the life we shared, so much more so than the many nights that have followed since I became his wife. We have been together for many years now, and when we make love it is good, but all the time two people inside us, the old Bálint and the old Irén, sit there at the end of the bed and register the same sardonic amusement that so disconcerted the witnesses at our wedding lunch. I sometimes wonder if it has ever crossed Bálint's mind that he is not my second husband but my third, and that I am in fact his second wife, not his first. The pair who married at the start of the 1960s were not a bachelor and a divorcée but a widow and a widower, the first of whom had been married briefly once before, the other twice: two people who no longer had any illusions about life or any expectations of it, but were simply unwilling to set off down the road to death, that difficult journey to make, alone. So if from time to time they found themselves in each other's embrace and "got along well enough," it was because each harbored the private memory of their first spouse, the true one, whose memory could never be erased: the Bálint Biró who had died along with Henriette and her parents, and the Irén Elekes, with her special smile, who was so loving and who had almost died at the same time.

So if one of them withdrew into silence, the other knew that he was remembering his first marriage, but she, being too weary to register the pain of that, and being older and wiser now, chose not to intrude on his recollections. But if she did have the strength at that particular moment, she might well retaliate in her own particular way. She could summon up memories of her own: what a fine head of hair you had then, and now you're going bald; what splendid blue eyes you had, and now you can't see properly without glasses; how very talented we all thought you were, and what a mediocrity you have turned out to be; but most of all, how inexpressibly I loved you then, and now the only thing that holds us together are these memories of Katalin Street...though it's true, of course, that they will stay with us until death.

That morning the Major was late.

The Major was never late, but these were exceptional times, and even when he still hadn't arrived, as he had promised, by nine o'clock, we thought little of it. In any case, we had to wait for the Helds. Henriette had told us that her father had gone to some office or other, taking all sorts of letters and documents with him, possibly so that he could do something for her grandparents, and of course when you went to these places they always kept you waiting. I longed for them to come back soon, because I wanted us to exchange rings straight after the lunch.

Meanwhile Henriette was tiptoeing around us in total silence, and this time it was her very tactfulness that annoyed me—wandering restlessly about from room to room and staring at my mother's cushions as if she had never seen them before, like some snotty-nosed sixteen-year-old who thought we were so desperate for a kiss that we couldn't wait for her to go home.

We chatted calmly enough until midday, when Bálint mentioned that his father had been told to report to command headquarters. Blanka suggested, rather hopefully, that he might buy some drinks on his way back because we were in short supply. My mother was still maintaining the uncharacteristic self-discipline she had shown at breakfast. My father took out a book and sat down under the bust of Cicero to read. Mrs. Temes, busying about in the kitchen, called for Henriette to come and help. Blanka was now back in the bedroom, furiously and audibly revising, and once again the two of us found ourselves alone. This time we did kiss, happily and passionately: my whole body was on fire.

At one point Henriette came in to ask Bálint what he thought might be the reason why her parents still hadn't arrived. He muttered something or other, not having grasped the point of her question. It was only after she had slunk timidly away that he called after her that it might have taken longer than usual to witness or copy some document. My heart beat so wildly I could hardly breathe. It was a moment of real triumph. For those few minutes I had reduced Bálint Bíró to total confusion.

One o'clock came and went, and still no sign of the Helds; only, at long last, the Major. That was wonderful, but what puzzled me was the odd way he let us know. He didn't come round and ring the bell; he went straight to his own house and phoned to ask us to send Bálint home.

"Something's up," Bálint observed. "I'll run over and see what it is."

I stared at him in horror. Run home? Leaving me here? At a time like this? Had his father gone mad? Henriette had been standing beside him, and when he left she did too. Noticing that she had followed him, Bálint stopped and shook his head.

"No, Henriette," he said. "Not you, just me. You stay here. I'll be back in a minute."

And off he went, leaving a difficult silence behind him, the sort of silence that follows when those remaining have no idea what has happened. I don't know what the others were thinking, but my concerns were that Bálint had gone without saying goodbye, our rings were still there on the table, and when would we get to put them on? At the same time I was sure there must be a perfectly natural explanation for all this: perhaps he and his father were preparing some special surprise.

It struck me that today I was the lady of the house, so I went up to Henriette: I could see how very worried she was. I wanted to pull her close to me and caress her, but she stepped back and stood looking out through the window into the garden, as if listening for something. But there was nothing to be heard.

By now my mother was reaching the end of her tether. Something very unusual had disrupted the plans for the day, and she doubtless felt that there was no longer any need to rein herself in. I watched as she kicked the shoe off her left foot and then, at a look from my father, put it reluctantly back on. Then she stood up. This was because Mrs. Temes had come in, carrying the bowl of chicken soup and setting it down on the dining-room table. She had gathered from what we were saying that the Major was back next door, he had been on the phone, he presumably had returned with the Helds, and it was time to serve lunch.

"Don't just stand there," my father said to Henriette. "Read something until it's served. A young girl should always be doing something." And he thrust a copy of *The Count of Monte Cristo* into her hand. Mrs. Temes continued bringing the food in, this time putting the salad bowl down on the sideboard. Blanka picked up a tiny lettuce leaf and offered it to Henriette, but she didn't want it and shook her head. She and I were the only two now standing. My father began to read the book he had offered to Henriette; my mother held her hand out behind her back and Blanka slipped the lettuce leaf into it without my father noticing. Mrs. Temes had vanished back into the kitchen.

The clang of the doorbell took us all by surprise. Blanka was the one who usually opened the door, but this time Henriette ran to get there first. "That's very thoughtful of her," I said to myself. "How quick she is." Only after that (and somewhat grudgingly) did I think, "It's because she's so frightened."

The three of them came in, and it was as if the sky had suddenly cleared. The room came to life, and everyone was smiling. The Major kissed me first, with Bálint and Henriette standing on either side of him. Henriette's face was radiant: she worshiped the Major. Bálint's eyes were turned on me and no one else: only me. He was trying to signal something to me with his eyes, but I couldn't think what it might be. I worked it out later, but at the time it seemed unimportant.

"Sadly, I can't stay for the lunch," the Major announced. "It's most regrettable, but there's nothing I can do about it. I have to leave you. Henriette must go with me. Her parents are waiting for her."

Henriette went pale. The Major put his hands on her shoulders and reassured her: "Now don't be silly. There's nothing to be afraid of. I met them in the street. They were with some old friends, people from the country. They're going to take you there, all three of you, very soon. It's bad luck that Bálint and Irén can't be going too. This never-ending bombing is really terrible. Now come, the car is waiting for you."

I believed him. Why should I not have? I couldn't understand why Henriette was behaving so oddly, standing there without moving. Was it because she would have to miss my engagement party?

"Say goodbye to the future bride," the Major went on. "We must hurry."

I stood and waited to see what would happen next. If the Helds were off to the country, they wouldn't be eating with us. The Major wouldn't either, because he was taking Henriette. There would be hardly anyone left. We'd done so much cooking there'd be enough for tomorrow.

Blanka dashed across and kissed Henriette. I should have done that, but I had been waiting to see if Bálint was going to stay or not. It was only when he didn't move, and didn't follow his father out of the room, that I rushed after her and kissed her too. I have no idea what she looked like when she turned back to glance at us briefly from the doorway. I still cannot recall that face.

My father was shaking his head, but my mother seemed both happy and relieved that neither the Major nor the Helds would be lunching with us. They always made her ill at ease, being so well turned out. Soon enough she had slipped off her shoes and started to hum a little tune. Blanka began to rearrange the table under Mrs. Temes's instructions, removing the now redundant place settings. I was watching Bálint to see if he would at last open the jewelry box. He hadn't so far. He hadn't even glanced at the rings.

Then it came: "The Helds have been taken away. My father saw it happen. Everyone who went to that office was taken. I'm sorry, but Henriette has to go with them. He's taking her there now."

My mother came out of the bedroom, still in her stockinged feet, and stopped in her tracks. The slippers fell from her hand. My father went pale, and his eyes filled with tears. Mrs. Temes slumped against the sideboard and bit her lip, her face a mass of red blotches. I stood there and tried to imagine it: Uncle and Auntie Held had been taken away, and now Henriette had to go with them. It just wasn't possible.

At that point Blanka burst into tears. My father put an arm round her and silently consoled her. I too should be crying, I thought. Bálint is waiting for me to cry. Years later he told me what he thought of me at the time, when he saw me standing there with eyes only for the two rings. But I couldn't cry.

"What kind of engagement party is this?" Blanka sobbed. "The poor Helds, I loved them so much, but if they were going to take them away, if they really had to, it should have been some other time. Not at Irén's engagement party."

Bálint turned to her and slapped her cheeks, both right and left. It was such an unexpected, frightening thing to do that my mother screamed. My father lowered his eyes. Mrs. Temes went to the kitchen without saying a word. I stared at Bálint, only at Bálint. I had no idea what was going on in his head. By then Blanka was no longer in the room.

WHEN THE moment did finally arrive, it came neither at the time nor in the manner she had anticipated and was altogether less dramatic. That it would come she had been sure, even if no one ever spoke about it. She was simply amazed that none of the others could see it coming as clearly as she did—not the Major, who was so wise and clever, or Bálint, who loved her so much, or the ever-sensible Mrs. Temes. They all seemed blind to anything that couldn't be seen or touched, things that were accessible only to the feelings. She often wondered too, if she was with any of them and they were talking to her, getting her to eat, trying to cheer her up and reassure her, why it was that they couldn't see that what was coming wasn't really important, wasn't worth the enormous risk the Major was taking, and that the precise manner of her removal from this world would be trivial compared to the fact itself. How could they not understand that she was in effect already dead?

She never put these questions to the Major, or Bálint, or Mrs. Temes. She could see what a source of comfort and reassurance her silence was to them, how little suspicion it aroused, and she remained exactly as they had always known her, gently submissive and amenable to instruction. Nor did she trouble them with questions about that mysterious place in the country where she had not been allowed to go with her parents when they left with their good friend so much sooner than expected, or to the place where they were waiting for her, in complete safety, until she too could safely leave the city, and it was really just a matter of a few days before she would be with them again.

"If you like, you could write to them," the Major had assured her just before he returned to the front. "Bálint will make sure it gets there." She thanked him and told him she didn't really want to.

During the previous two weeks, after exploring all the possibilities, the Helds had finally settled on a password that, if they were separated, would tell the family member receiving it that they were alive and safe, or at least that the sender was. The Major had not once used that word, he clearly wasn't aware of it, so Henriette knew that her parents had been arrested. She felt truly sorry for Bálint, at his wits' end trying to find ways to distract her and having to leave her with Mrs. Temes when he failed or when his work kept him at the hospital overnight. Mrs. Temes couldn't always be with her either: shopping was difficult, and she often had to wait in line for hours. Henriette was forbidden to go into the garden, and there was only one situation in which she should ever leave the house. Before he left, the Major had been very precise in his instructions as to what those circumstances might be.

She was never bored. In fact it seemed to her that time was racing by. Every so often she would glance anxiously at her watch. It always told her that it was later than she had thought—no sooner had morning arrived than it was evening. If Bálint was at home the two of them would play cards, talk about this and that, and listen to the radio. He would play the piano, or they would rummage through their boxes of

games to see what there was for two people to play, three if
Mrs. Temes was around. When Bálint wasn't there, Mrs.
Temes got her to cook lunch or bake cakes. She played or
worked according to their wishes, but none of these activities
brought her the same sense of peace as when she was truly
on her own, without other people trying to make her life
easier by their presence. She could certainly think of greater
sources of comfort than the exaggerated reassurances of Mrs.
Temes, or even the foreign-language broadcasts which she
could understand but to which she listened as if they had
nothing to do with her, though they gave her more hope
than Bálint did. When he was physically present she was
incapable of thinking about anything other than what he
wanted, but it was also important for her to set aside time
every day to think about those things that did bring her
strength and peace of mind: her various deaths.

It was a comfort to know that she had died at least one
natural death, one that every other young girl before her
must have experienced, and not just the one that was clearly
going to happen when she was sixteen. So whenever her
parents talked about their chances of escape and survival
she went and sat with them and looked back over her memories, always returning to the one in which she saw herself
breathing her last in the garden, the Elekeses' garden, where
she had died on her feet, like a soldier, without flinching, as
do the brave. "Bálint is going to marry Irén," Blanka had
said, dancing from side to side. Henriette looked at her and
said nothing. She was holding her watch—she had just started
to wind it—but the action was frozen in midair, and she
stood there as still as a painting of herself holding a watch.
What astonished her most was her own astonishment, when
it had been so obvious that one day this would happen, as

was the fact that she was the only one who really loved Bálint and that Bálint didn't love her. Well of course he did, but not in the same way, not in the way that would make it enough for her to want to stay among the living. "My life is over," she reflected in wonderment. She considered it at length, how simply it had occurred, quite unconnected with all those wartime announcements or the new laws and restrictions that were being passed by the authorities every day. Her father had put his trust in his medals from the Great War and her mother had talked about God. How she would have loved to comfort them, to tell them that when the day came when neither prayers nor military honors would save them, at least they wouldn't have to mourn for her as well because she would already be long dead.

Years before, when they were still children, they had played a great many games—their parents thought it would be good for them, at least those that could be confined to a garden or an enclosed yard. She always asked for the Cherry Tree, even years after she ought to have been just a little ashamed to do so. It exerted a powerful and inexplicable charm over her. Bálint hated the game, but he did sometimes consent to take part. He was always the one in the middle, and he always chose Irén as his partner, while she and Blanka stood on either side and clapped their hands as the pair went spinning round and round between them. Henriette knew that everything that had happened to her, and perhaps was still waiting to happen, flowed, perhaps even before the coming of Hitler, from that game in the garden, the Cherry Tree game, in which Bálint always chose Irén.

The second time she experienced a death she again did so silently and without any visible reaction, and this made her feel that perhaps the final one wasn't too greatly to be feared either. The Major had taken her to his house and gone through the motions of telephoning someone before announcing that, owing to some misunderstanding, her parents had traveled on ahead and that she would have to stay with him for the time being, until the next car was due to leave. She loved and missed her parents intensely, but she knew at once that they had been arrested and that she would never see them again. What she felt then was something no tears could assuage. "They will be killed," she thought, when the Major finally left her alone in the room. "They will know no more fear, and nothing can harm them again; and I have died with them, because they alone knew what I am like when I let myself be as I really am. Irén and Blanka have never seen anything of my true self, because I have never had the courage to reveal it to them: I always had the feeling that, however much they were part of my life, they were inside a closed circle and I was on the outside. And there was something the Major and Bálint couldn't see either: that I always made a special effort when I was with them because I so wanted to belong, to be part of their safe and confident world. I was like a homeless puppy, offering myself to them, in my own quiet way, because I loved Bálint so unutterably."

So she went along with the idea of her parents' departure, the fiction that they really had traveled to some place where she would soon follow them. Sometimes when they had gone on a family holiday to Lake Balaton her mother would indeed travel on ahead to sort out the accommodation. "So, yes," she said to herself, "they really are waiting for me." And she spent hours daydreaming about when and how it would be when they did meet again.

Strangely enough, it was only the third death that provoked her tears. It was the least meaningful of the three. It changed nothing, it taught her nothing new, but it upset her more because the way it happened was so childish and for that reason all the more shocking. The Major had explained to her very carefully what she should do if they heard the bell ring and Mrs. Temes opened the door to anyone. If Mrs. Temes then went into the garden and stood beside the fountain and complained loudly about the difficulty of finding provisions, Henriette should go quickly and at once up to the attic above his late wife's bedroom, where they had put her, because it meant that the visitor wanted to see something in one of the rooms; if Mrs. Temes complained about the slowness of the mail or the frequency of the bombing, she was to go down to the cellar, where there was a hiding place behind a stack of coal; and if Mrs. Temes talked about a pharmacy or referred to an illness, then she should go out into the garden, go round behind the hedge, which was now tall and thickly overgrown, and make her way to the tall fence between the Biró garden and her own. Bálint had removed enough nails from some of the panels to make a gap wide enough for her to slip through, and he had done the same on the Elekes side as well; so if she heard Mrs. Temes mention a pharmacy or an illness, she should pass along behind that second hedge—it was just as dense and overgrown as in the other gardens—and make her way as quickly as she could behind her old garden and down into the cellar in the Elekes house.

She had been at the Major's for just a week when the doorbell rang. Mrs. Temes went outside and stood beside the fountain, talking to two strangers, a man and a woman. From behind the curtain she could see them clearly and could hear what they were saying: they were looking for rooms to accommodate people whose homes had been bombed.

Mrs. Temes said something about the terrible difficulty of finding rations, and told them that the Major's house had been exempt from the new controls. The woman replied they would still have to register it in case there was an emergency and it became absolutely necessary to put people in there. Henriette ran from the room and up the wooden staircase, and had reached the secret place behind the huge traveling trunks when she suddenly stopped. She stood stock-still, forgetting her instructions: from up there in the attic she could see out into her garden. She had a good view of her back door, which led down onto the grass, and there on the steps were the bottle for pickling cucumbers, some cucumbers sliced in half, and some bread her mother had put out to dry in the sun. At the far end, her swing moved gently in the wind. Otherwise the garden was empty. The flowers hadn't been watered and were bone-dry.

She stood and wept so bitterly that she thought she must have been heard down below and she struggled desperately to pull herself together; but the sight of those cucumbers, the watering can, and the swing kept the tears flowing. They stood for everything that had happened. She had no house, no home, no family; even her name was no longer her own: if anyone asked she was to say she was Mária Kis, her father was Antal Kis and her mother Nora Müller. On the two previous occasions, first when she had finally grasped that Bálint was to be engaged to Irén, and then when she realized that she would never see either her father or her mother again, and what that meant, the emotion had been just too brutal, something that tears could never express. But now, in the minutes preceding her third death, she finally understood the mute power of physical objects and everything they could stand for.

On the day it happened Bálint wasn't with her. He had been able only to promise that he would be back from the hospital some time that evening. Mrs. Temes had been instructed by the Major to carry on with her life as if things were perfectly normal, and she had been out shopping with her ration vouchers. Henriette had tried to read and had listened to the radio. Mrs. Temes came back rather late and in a bad mood, and for a while bustled about in silence. Henriette knew what this meant. When Mrs. Temes moved about the house without saying a word it meant she was worried and upset about something. She saw her trying to telephone Bálint—she actually got through to the hospital but was unable to reach him. Henriette heard her try three times, but she was now hearing other noises too, very close to hand, a dull, heavy thudding, as if objects of some size were being dumped on the ground somewhere. Finally Mrs. Temes came into the room and told her what she had seen while she was out. The army or some such organization had commandeered the Held house and were taking out the furniture, throwing everything into the garden; she had asked the sentry standing at the door what they were going to do with the building and he had told her it was to be a first-aid center and an emergency hospital: the city was full of people injured in the bombing and in desperate need of attention.

Henriette looked at her in astonishment. How could this woman, who had known her since the age of six, be so incapable of imagining what was going on in her head, and how could two people react to things so very differently? It was now clear to her that if she ever needed to leave the house they would have to devise a new plan, because, if her former home was to be turned into a first-aid center, from the next morning onwards it would no longer be possible in an emergency to get to the Elekes house by way of her old garden. Did that really matter? Bálint would decide: he had already told her that they wouldn't be keeping her in the house for very long.

Mrs. Temes was equally puzzled: didn't the girl understand what had happened, or was she so indifferent to everything that was going on that she hadn't been paying attention? Bálint would have to take her away that very night. If there were a full-scale aerial or artillery attack they would have to vacate the house, and everyone in the street knew Henriette. Even though the Major was away at the front he would be in serious trouble.

Henriette left the room. When she got to the wooden staircase she took her shoes off so that Mrs. Temes wouldn't hear where she was going, slipped into the attic, as she had done earlier that day, and looked out. The garden down below was swarming with soldiers. All their furniture—beds, tables, the sideboard, chairs, the contents of drawers, books, and even underwear—had been taken out, dumped in heaps among the roses, and was in the process of being sorted. She could see her dresses, her school satchel, all the familiar objects of her life in full view, out there in the garden. Her father's white shirts were strewn over an armchair. But none of his instruments seemed to be there, so the surgery must have been left untouched.

She stood there motionless, looking at what was left of her past. Every item there had its own history, though the soldiers moving between them knew none of it: objects have nothing to say to strangers. The soldiers worked quickly, almost professionally. Nothing was slipped into pockets, everything was being sorted into appropriate categories, chairs with chairs, pictures with pictures, smaller items into baskets, bedding, underwear, and bed linen into a separate pile. Henriette thought of the different smells, the fragrance of the pillows, the white coats fresh from the laundry or smelling of starch—and the towels, the soft touch of the towels. Everything was falling apart, the house was disintegrating before her eyes, reverting to its component parts; for her, whose home it had been, everything that had ever happened to those objects lived on in that jumbled pile of things that meant nothing to the people handling them.

Mrs. Temes wouldn't come looking for her, she was sure. She would be reading a book or preparing supper. So she stayed where she was until the last soldier had gone. It was getting dark and the lights in the house were on when she finally went down to supper.

They were about to start on the stewed fruit when the doorbell rang twice and then twice again, the family code. One of Mrs. Temes's relatives.

"Go to your room," Mrs. Temes ordered. "Take your bowl of fruit with you. Be quick!"

She obeyed and went out, spilling some juice as she climbed the stairs. At the bend she paused before going into her room, to hear who had come. It was Mrs. Temes's niece. She always stayed for ages, talking nonstop—Henriette had known her ever since she lived in the street. She put her bowl down on the little sideboard on the landing and continued on her way up to the attic. The moon was high in the sky, but from up there she could see very little now.

"Those laundry smells," she said to herself. "Among the pillows, on the bedspread, on our clothes—the only memorial to Nagy Anna and Lajos Held." And that barely perceptible indentation on the sofa where she and her father had always sat together reading...and a tangle of towels, her head bent forward with her hair falling in front of her, her mother rubbing briskly to make it dry faster, laughing as she rubbed. Henriette was already dead, but even in her hour of death she wanted to see it again, the place where she had once lived. She ran down the stairs and out through the back door into the garden.

The Major's house was in complete darkness. There was no light coming through the shutters, so she knew that neither Mrs. Temes or her niece would see her as she ran down the gravel path and past the fountain with the bronze fish toward the hedge. The sky stretched wide above her head; pale moonlight picked out the trees and the ragged outline of the hedge. Reaching the hedge, she slipped through, ran along to the fence and located the loosened boards. She undid them and slid past. And there, in her own garden at last, in the shadow of its trees and surrounded by the heady scent of its flowers, she sat down on the grass and buried her head in her hands.

"Those fragrances," she thought. "Just this once more, for the last time, and never again . . . from deep inside the pillows, as in a dream." She stood up and went over to the stacks of furniture, to the pile she was looking for—the white coats, the pillows, and the towels—then knelt on the ground in front of them, nestled her head against the pillows, and inhaled deeply, as if panting for breath.

After some time she rose to her feet. As she did so she stumbled against the eighteenth-century footstool, the one with the shepherd and shepherdess standing on either side of a stream, the girl with a beribboned stick and a jug and the boy lifting his hat in greeting. The footstool fell over with a dull crash.

A light flickered in the doorway for a moment and instantly went out: a ray of blue light, the blue flicker of an electric flashlight. Someone shouted—a long sentence, clearly enunciated, impossible to misunderstand. Not so much frightened as caught off guard, Henriette scrambled to her feet and began to run toward the fence on the left-hand side. As she reached the archway she heard the soldier shout again, and she was struck by the absurd thought of how sensible it was that they had left a watchman at the deserted house in case people might steal something: a house in that situation really needed one.

She made it to the hedge, still much less afraid than she would have expected. Now for the Elekes house! Irén had prepared a hiding place in the cellar, which was never locked. The soldier would have spent some time looking for her and wondering where she had gone. Reaching the fence, she started to push on the two boards that Bálint had loosened to let her through to the Elekeses' garden, and her heart came to a stop. The boards refused to budge. They had been nailed back on the other side.

Completely forgetting that she should always stay behind the hedge, she ran blindly into the garden, towards the Birós' fence that she had come in through. Another flash of blue light. It didn't reach her, but the soldier was now in the garden. At that point she knew how wrong she had been earlier: she hadn't died on either the first or the second occasion, or even on this the third. She was still alive, and she wanted to live. But by the time she realized that she was already dead.

Two shots rang out in the moonlight. Searching unsuccessfully by the light of his torch, the soldier decided his aim had been poor. But the first bullet had flown true to its mark.

I HAVE already described what sort of people we were, so you will understand why I was the only one the Major and Bálint had told the truth to about where Henriette was, and why the rest of the family simply accepted the official version, that she had gone to join her parents and they had left Budapest. My mother was incapable of keeping a secret, so much so that we had to hide our Christmas presents at the Helds': the moment she suspected that we had bought her something she would immediately put aside her constitutional idleness and start searching for it, turning the entire house upside down in her desperation to see what it was and completely destroying its value as a gift for a special occasion. With Blanka there was a different problem. She was so riddled with fear, so terrified of the war and of being hurt or harmed in any way, that we couldn't risk her knowing anything. Though she loved Henriette like a sister, we could never be sure that if she were ever questioned, or actually threatened, she wouldn't simply burst into tears and blurt out the truth to make them leave her alone and stop tormenting her, only to realize a few minutes later that what she had just done might have sent someone to their death. Nor could we put the least reliance on my father. He quite understood that the Helds were in an exceptional situation, and that it was natural and proper for the Major to do everything in his power to help them, but on the other hand it was actually illegal to hide such people, the law expressly forbade it, and respect for the laws of the land—even the most immoral of them—ran as deep in him as the marrow in his bones. The sort of things that were going on at that time filled him with astonishment and dismay. Both as a Christian and a teacher whose vocation was to instill moral values in the community, he rejected the beliefs and attitudes of the fascists. But for him obedience to authority, submission to one's superiors, in whatever circumstances and however painful, remained an absolute duty. It would take the death of the Helds and the disappearance of Henriette to smash his brittle morality to pieces. Even today he cannot forgive himself for what followed—and now of course he is in a position to help no one.

Bálint came over to see us later, that evening of the day of our engagement. It seemed perfectly natural. It had been a very sad day: Uncle Held was obviously no longer protected by his medals and it had been necessary to intern the two of them for a while in some sort of detention camp—or so my father thought and believed; but we exchanged rings nonetheless. We went out into the garden, this time without Blanka, and Bálint chose the bench farthest from the windows to deliver his message, in a terse whisper: Henriette was still with us, she was to stay at their house until they could find somewhere for her to go; the Major would be returning to the front the following day but Mrs. Temes could be depended upon, and as the house was the home of a serving soldier, it was unlikely to be troubled by the authorities and she could hide there in safety. If he could contrive a way, he would come for her in an ambulance, take her to the hospital, and hide her among the patients under the name of Mária Kis. If the Helds hadn't gone off in such a hurry but had waited for his father—who of course hadn't been summoned to headquarters but had gone to try and get them false documents—they wouldn't have ended up in that accursed office where everyone who presented themselves was detained, and he would have been able to save them.

Bálint added that he would go to the Helds' later that night and loosen some of the fencing planks in both their garden and ours, so that if their house were ever searched or hit by a bomb Henriette would be able to run through their garden to ours and hide in the cellar: it was the last place anyone ever went to, and one we knew well from our childhood games. I was not to go to the university. I was to stay at home and wait in case I could be of help. All that, without arousing the suspicion of the rest of the family.

He spoke slowly and precisely. There was none of the low, gentle murmuring of a fiancé—these were orders. I listened attentively but my mind was racing. He couldn't spare me even this one evening, on this very special day: once again he was interested only in Henriette and keeping her safe. He hadn't even kissed me. I knew he had been in love with me for many years, but now something between us had broken. At the same time I was furious with myself for being so base and selfish on the day the Helds had been arrested and Henriette's life put in danger. Was I simply jealous of the concern he was showing for her? "I'm the one he loves," I consoled myself, and later on we did exchange a kiss. But somehow it wasn't the same. The shadow of the Helds hung over us, and I was thinking that now Henriette was going to be living with Bálint and the Major. Mrs. Temes lodged downstairs, in a separate part of the house, so they would be alone on the first floor, and what might happen then?

Nothing—I felt sure of it. Nothing at all. They both loved me. Only now do I see that the reason for my hard feelings toward Henriette was that she had managed to awaken something in Bálint that went beyond both love and desire.

The night following my engagement was a troubled one: I simply couldn't rest. Blanka sniffled and sobbed for a while, then fell asleep. It was a long time before I went to bed. I stood at the window leaning on the sill and staring out into the garden, as I had done that same morning. I was thinking that Henriette would now be sleeping under the same roof as Bálint before I would.

The Major (I never addressed him as "father," I never had the chance—he was killed just a few weeks after our engagement) went back the next morning, and Bálint spent almost the whole day at the hospital. As I had promised, I didn't go to the university. I told my father the lie that I had nothing to do there because the courses had been suspended due to the bombing raids. Blanka was busy cramming, and the days seemed endless. I saw Henriette only once, and even then she didn't know I had.

It was building up for rain, and clouds covered the moon. It was a particularly mild evening. After supper I went out into the garden, moved the loosened boards aside, and slipped through into the Helds' deserted property. I wasn't afraid, just very sad. In the silence and darkness the house seemed no more real than the ruins of Pompeii, which I saw some years later on a group holiday. If at that moment some spirit, one of those guardian angels whose sole duty is to accompany one's footsteps through life and inspire both good and bad thoughts (so a *good* spirit in this case), had whispered in my ear that I should go back home and, despite the prohibition, tell my father—because he was an honorable man, even if currently in a state of moral paralysis after discovering that the law he had upheld all his life can itself be illegal—that Bálint was hiding Henriette...then perhaps everything would have turned out differently, and perhaps our life together now might have been rather better than it is, because, as I now know, everything changed for us with the death of Henriette.

But the spirit standing behind me was an evil one. It urged me to go deeper into the Major's garden to see what was happening there. Once we were married it would be my home anyway, not Henriette's; and besides, Bálint was late, he should have been at our house some time before this, because when I had phoned the hospital a little while before they had said he had gone home "much earlier."

So I pushed aside the planks in the Birós' fence and continued on my way behind the hedge, keeping my head well down. The ground was soft underfoot—Mrs. Temes must have been out watering the garden. The first thing that caught my eye was Bálint, sitting in the semidarkness on the edge of the stone fountain, with Henriette beside him. I stopped and waited. I have no idea what I was hoping for. We often don't know what we really want.

The evening was so soft I felt I could grasp the air, the wind, or the shadows in my hand. Of the house itself I could see very little. I often dream about the total darkness of the blackout: I see the blanked-out windows, and it sometimes makes me cry. When this happens, Bálint wakes me up by shaking my shoulders, but he never asks me why I am crying, and I never tell him. There seems no point.

They were talking quietly but I could clearly make out what they were saying. Mrs. Temes wasn't with them, but I knew where she was because I could hear her singing—the lilt of a folk song was coming from behind the shutters in the kitchen. For a moment it shocked me once again that they should have entrusted Henriette to her and not to us: only later did it seem really hurtful.

Their shadows merged, making the two of them look like a single person. Bálint was speaking, calling her by the name he had sometimes used when they were children and he wanted to tease her. For some reason it had really upset her then, but now it was "Henrik" once again and I had the feeling that this time she didn't mind at all, in fact she was enjoying it, as a term of endearment. When my Kinga was born, and I was a new and happy mother living apart from the world and from people, this was the voice I used with my baby daughter, the one Bálint was using with Henriette now. There is a kind of speech in which the words themselves become a mere framework, a sequence of vowels and consonants so charged with feeling that their literal meaning becomes irrelevant.

"Henrik," I heard him say in the semidarkness, "silly little Henrik will put on her pretty blue dress and we'll take her to see the whole wide world. We'll take her to Salzburg and listen to Mozart, and little Henrik will sit in the front row and clap her hands, and then she'll go to Paris to see the paintings and the statues, and she'll go to all the other places too. She will wear her pretty white hat and her patent leather shoes, and her gloves will be tied around her neck, because little Henrik is still very little and she loses everything, and if she loses her gloves they won't let her in to meet the pope in Rome, which would be so sad, because he really wants to see her and say to her, 'Young lady, if only I were able to marry....'"

I didn't catch what she said in reply, but she did say something. I only heard her laugh, and after that I had no more wish to listen. Bálint never spoke in that way with me. He just kissed me and stroked my breasts. Until that moment I had not realized how little he actually gave me, and I wanted some of what Henriette had been given.

I made my way home through the Helds' garden. The family had been looking for me. I just muttered something and went and sat down to wait for him in the morning room, wondering what he was going to say. He came at nine. I reckoned he must have given silly little Henrik her supper and she was now playing dominoes with Mrs. Temes. They were certainly doing their best to keep her amused. I ran to meet him, and we kissed in the entrance hall.

I prayed desperately that he wouldn't lie to me. I wanted him to say, "Irén, I didn't want to leave Henriette alone this evening, so I spent some time sitting with her in the garden." Instead he looked at me as if he were weighing up what he should say. Then he kissed me again, and said he'd had a difficult evening in the hospital, had spent hours sitting with a patient, and had just arrived home. I nodded, as if I understood. He stayed for dinner. I noticed how hungry he was, and I thought, no doubt he gives his own food to silly little Henrik, because officially she doesn't exist and Mária Kis won't have a ration book.

Please don't get me wrong: I loved Henriette and I really wanted her to live. To live for a thousand years, and for life to make up to her for our wicked laws and for everything that had happened to her and to all the Helds, and also because of that nameless something that had made Bálint lie to me and sit there with her on the edge of the fountain with the gasping fish and promise that he would take her to Salzburg and that the pope would fall in love with her. But understand this too: behind the thoughts that were in my mind was another set of preoccupations of a different order altogether, thoughts that were buried so deep in me that I had never realized they were there. They knew it was better to stay unformulated and never rise into consciousness, but they were there just the same, watching and waiting.

On the morning of the day when the Helds' house was emptied by the military or whoever it was, before being converted into a first-aid station, I had a truly horrible row with Blanka. Once again she had taken something of mine and ruined it, and the stress I was under from my thoughts about Bálint and Henriette's relationship, added to the shame I felt at not being able to be more reasonable and less envious of the few kind words she'd had from Bálint, led to an explosion. You could buy stockings only with coupons, and on the previous day Blanka had gone to have her graduation photograph taken: she was desperate to look pretty, so she selected my very best pair, the ones I had first worn on the day of my engagement and, as she explained later between her sobs, taken them "with your subsequent permission," because she didn't have a single pair of her own. On the bus someone had given her a kick, and she had brought them back with a large hole in them. I saw it only in the morning when I went to put them on. Naturally, she hadn't dared show them to me.

It is always the most inexplicable things that make us lose self-control. Clearly it wasn't the stockings that had made me so upset, but I wept and raged so bitterly that my father came rushing in anxiously to see what the matter was. Blanka was staring at me, her lips quivering, her eyes wide with fear, as they always were on these occasions. She was holding out her tiny horseshoe-shaped purse—there was hardly anything in it, but it was all the little she had—and wanting me to take it all, down to the last penny, as a punishment: she was so much to blame, so useless. Gradually I calmed down, stopped crying, and put the ruined stockings back in the drawer. By the time I was telling her to pull herself together I was relatively collected myself. I told her that I simply couldn't abide the perpetual chaos and filth that reigned in the house because of her and my mother. Rose had gone, and my father and I had to do everything; I couldn't tell my mother what to do, but Blanka at least, if she wanted to live in peace with me, would have to stop doing things that annoyed me. She was so untidy I couldn't bear to live with her a moment longer. At least she might try, as a break from studying, to pick up one or two things occasionally and not just leave it all to me. If she wanted me to forget what she had done to the stockings, she could spread a little order and cleanliness around her. That very day she had once again hung her underwear out in the garden, the way the Gypsies do; she'd had the nerve to tie a rope between two shrubs and string up her slips there, because she was too lazy to go up to the attic. It was a disgrace to behold. She had better get them out of the garden immediately or I didn't know what I would do to her. She went out without saying a word.

We had lunch together. She had arranged to go to a school friend's house to revise her physics work and came home several hours after I had gone out myself, contrary to Bálint's instructions. I had been required to attend a course for air-raid wardens, and absence was a punishable offense. I returned just as supper was being served. Blanka was very quiet, hardly daring to speak to me. Finally she told me she had cooked the meal. I was very pleased about that, because she was a much better cook than my mother. On her right hand there was a bandage, a really squalid, disgusting bandage, that she was obviously eager that I should see—I didn't ask her how she came by it because she so much wanted me to. These accidents were an everyday occurrence: she was forever cutting, burning, or scalding herself when she cooked.

Meanwhile Bálint hadn't even phoned. I tried to get him at the hospital, only to be told he was there somewhere but they couldn't trace him. I really wanted to talk to him, to tell him what was happening at the Helds' house, and I urgently wanted him to come home early and talk to me, now that we needed to revise his plans for Henriette's safety. The morning's explosion over the stockings had resolved something inside me, and I was now deeply ashamed of having made such a ridiculous fuss about them. Blanka started to clear the table, and my father ordered me to help her: couldn't I see how awkward she was, with her bandaged hand?

She was in the kitchen, struggling. I went and relieved her of the work. She was holding her left hand against the bandage and could neither wash nor dry things properly. Thinking of her terrified face that morning and the way she had held out her purse for me to take suddenly made me laugh. My good angel was standing behind me, whispering gentle words in my ear, and I offered her my cheek. She understood at once that I was no longer angry with her, hugged and kissed me and put her arms around my neck, then she grabbed the footstool and sat down on it. Her face was radiant. While I had been out on my course, both in the morning and the afternoon, and even during her breaks from revising, everything had been left for her to do, and she was overjoyed not to have to do any more that night. She smiled at me, cosseted her bandaged hand, and the words began to flow.

She told me what a good girl she had been, how hard she had studied, and she had also cooked the supper and tidied the rooms: see how clean it was everywhere! And then she had another surprise for me, because I had scolded her so harshly that morning and told her how lazy and untidy she was.

Blanka's surprises! I took a fresh tea towel and carried on working in silence. She unpicked the bandage with her free fingers and showed me her hand. It was revolting. There was a deep, ugly wound ripped into the flesh: not the sort of injury you would come by in a kitchen.

"I did the garden as well," she beamed. "You were angry about the drying line so I took it down. I worked like a slave the whole afternoon, while you were out on your course. I cut the grass; I tidied up behind the hedge. I even swept it. It's really tidy now."

"About time too," I said, and carried on working.

"I also hammered the nails in," she went on, and pointed to her hand once again. "That's what did this. But I hammered them all back in."

"Which nails?" I asked. I wasn't in the least bit interested. I was chatting with her simply out of politeness and a sense of guilt because I had given the poor girl such an earful that morning.

"The loose ones in the fence," she replied, and gazed at me with the expression of a puppy yearning for praise. "I nailed them all back."

The dish fell from my hand, and the crash mingled with the shouting outside, and the two gunshots that followed immediately after.

THE CLANG of the doorbell made her start, and the now familiar sense of despair flooded over her once again. There was no one she could rely on: only herself. In this family of four people she lived like an orphan, entirely alone. When anything went wrong she could never behave as naturally as she would want. There was always someone in a bad mood, someone needing to be nursed or comforted. From this not even her father was exempt. So deeply ingrained had been his conviction that his life's work was based on an unshakable moral foundation and that the truth, after however many trials and tribulations, must eventually triumph, that he was now in a state of collapse. Week after week his ideas and ideals were undermined—statesmen reneged on agreements made only the day before, citizens lost their rights from one day to the next, fully grown adults hurled incendiary bombs into hospitals for mewling babies at the breast. When the Helds were deported it was almost more than he could bear, but after the killing of Henriette—though he never could understand how she came to be in her old garden—he completely lost his balance. Irén watched him searching for a tranquilizer, then standing for ages staring at the tablet in his hand, both hand and tablet shaking as in an earthquake.

Irén's mind reacted to Henriette's death as if one of her

limbs had been anesthetized: the thought had sliced through her like a scalpel, but she felt the pain only later. After Mrs. Temes left, Blanka had taken to following Irén around with a tear-streaked face, explaining over and over again the very circumstances she most wanted to forget. Now Irén had sent her off to their bedroom and her little sister was lying there, dabbing her eyes with a towel, blowing her nose and using her one free hand to torment her childhood teddy bear, which even at this age she still kept on the table beside her bed. Irén desperately wanted to be alone, to lock herself in the bathroom, so that no one could make her feelings even more painful by talking about their own. But Blanka was forever wanting something from her or asking her questions. At one point she felt she could stand it no longer and was on the point of screaming at her, "Quiet, you murderer!"

Once again her mother was proving the least of her problems. In exceptional circumstances she always produced exceptional behavior, as on the day of the engagement when she had worn those tight shoes because they looked so pretty, had eaten so beautifully at breakfast, and generally attempted to conduct herself in a dignified manner. On this occasion she had wept for a few minutes, then quite impartially and almost without emotion, but in the most obscene language imaginable, heaped curses on those responsible. Her husband blanched and fled to his study, fighting down his nausea: in his house even such innocent words as "shucks" or "damn" were forbidden, and hearing his wife uttering these obscenities, picked up from God knows where and stored inside her head for just this occasion, made him almost physically sick. She then took herself off to bed at her usual hour and promptly fell asleep. She was the only member of the family who never had difficulty sleeping. She would go to bed even when it was almost certain that there would be another air raid. She had been formed by nature for long, sleep-filled nights, and when she was woken up to be taken to the shelter she would be furious: how dare they involve her in their brainless military escapades and pluck her from her warm bed to go down to the cellar! She was so incensed she forgot to be afraid.

Irén looked for things to do. She tidied up. She wrapped things up into parcels, not quite knowing why. There was no question of going to bed—to end the day as if it had been just like any other was unthinkable.

Mr. Elekes had also stayed up, long after he had taken his pill, sitting under the bust of Cicero, paging through some old exercise books. He had personally taught the Held girl in one of the elementary classes and had kept some of her work in his special collection. Irén couldn't bear to watch him searching through those meticulously bound exercise books as if looking for a reason why she had to be shot at the age of sixteen. In due course the tranquilizer overcame him, and when the doorbell rang he was slumped over the desk with his head resting on Henriette's homework.

She tried to shake him awake, without success. He looked up briefly and promptly shut his eyes again. She could hear her mother's snores coming from the bedroom. Blanka was still up and fully dressed, but she could expect nothing from her. Ever since the start of the war and the raids, Blanka had been so filled with fear once night fell that whenever the doorbell rang she would try to hide, and in the most stupid of places, the bathroom or the larder. Irén went quickly to the front door and stood waiting and listening before she slid the bolt. She breathed a jumbled, wordless prayer, addressed not to God but, for some strange reason, to Henriette, pleading that whoever stood on the other side of the door might not be Bálint. Anyone but Bálint.

The harsh clang sounded again. Otherwise the silence outside was total. No clink of jostled weaponry, no muttering voices: not a raid, then. Another hope—a naïve one, but she clung to it—if not a raid, let it be a passing drunk. Or a child, someone trying to frighten them or drive them away. Why should people not want to play practical jokes even in 1944?

She knew of course that it was Bálint. Not just because he hadn't taken his finger off the button, and that sort of impatience and display of urgency was so typical of him, but because it would be so much in keeping with the rest of her day. She called out to ask who was there, and when there was no reply she opened the door.

He must have come straight from home, having seen Mrs. Temes: she could see from his face that he knew what had happened. For a while they stood there, face-to-face, like two actors the director has told not to step either toward each other or back but to stand close enough to feel each other's breath. Then he closed the door and pulled Irén to him. For the first few seconds his touch wasn't that of a grown man. In their childhood they had often stood thus when one of them was upset or cold and the other wanted to comfort or to warm them. This contact was as if they weren't sexual beings but simply seeking warmth, as they had done so many years before. Then, as if their intertwined bodies had suddenly remembered that they were now a man and a woman, they were overcome by a blind mutual desire. In those moments they were not conscious of themselves or each other but of Henriette and her death. They clung to each other and kissed as if a chasm had opened up before them and they were clinging to one another to stop the other person from plunging into the void. She realized later that at that moment, there in the doorway, she should have told Bálint everything—the air warden's course, the boards that had been nailed back, and the part she and Blanka had played in Henriette's death. Then perhaps everything would have turned out differently. But she said nothing. She was too afraid. Later again she realized that there was only one person who would have had the courage to tell the truth, had she known it, and that person was Blanka.

They went into the house. Nothing was said; there was nothing to say. From the account Mrs. Temes had given her of Henriette's death she could guess what he believed had happened: that in spite of all those instructions and the promises she had made, Henriette had obviously wanted to bid farewell to her former home, had run across their garden, and the guard on duty had seen her and shot her before she could reach the Elekeses' fence. Bálint began walking around the house. Irén knew this habit of his of going from room to room, but she noticed that it wasn't with the casual familiarity of someone who had known the place from childhood. At first she was puzzled by the difference from his usual way of moving about. This was a man who never pulled out drawers or barged into a room without knocking: now he was sauntering around. He took one glance at Mr. Elekes, who was completely unconscious, casually brushed some papers from the desk with his elbow, and went into the darkened bedroom where Mrs. Elekes's snufflings could be heard. There was something altogether inhuman and bewildering in this wandering. He even went into the girls' room, but he didn't find Blanka, only her made-up bed. Irén knew no more than he did where she was hiding—perhaps behind the curtain or under the bed itself. Even if Blanka had realized it was Bálint she would never have dared to come out. She would have been too embarrassed to be seen in her nightdress.

Irén had no idea what he was looking for, but he was certainly looking for something. She was tense, unhappy, and very tired, and she would have loved to go to bed at last, or simply get away. But it was impossible: Bálint was not making anything easy for her. He looked in the larder. Thinking he might be hungry she reached out for some bread, but he shook his head. In a corner behind the tub of pickled cabbage he found the siphon for drawing wine and took it with him as a sort of walking stick. She stared at him in amazement as he went, a man in uniform with an empty glass siphon under his arm. Seeing that he was determined to press on, she went and stood in front of him. He pushed her back—not as a lover might but almost roughly. There was no suggestion in his movements now of gentleness or desire. On he went, wine siphon in hand, moving from room to room, until at last he opened the door into the garden and went out into the courtyard. She followed him, once again racking her brains to think what he might be after. When he opened the door that led down to the network of cellars she felt momentarily reassured. She particularly loved the shelter they had made at the far end of it: cut deep into the rock of the Castle walls, it gave her a real sense of security. At least down there they might enjoy a few minutes of private conversation. She knew it would have to be brief: even though they were engaged her father would never allow her to be in there alone with him. But she followed him all the same.

She called out to him. He mumbled something indistinct,

more like a snarl, and walked on. He yanked open the door to the wine cellar, switched on the light, and carried on down the long passageway so quickly she had to run to keep up. As she drew alongside him, she noticed not just the uniformed figure but the strange expression on his face, the unfamiliar gestures and movements, the odd-looking close-cut hair on the back of his neck, and she suddenly realized that the man she had let into the house was not Bálint but a soldier. He had known her since birth, he knew everyone in the family, the house itself and every item of furniture in it, and here he was, pulling drawers open, poking around in their larder, and barging into their wine cellar the moment he felt thirsty. She stood behind him, watching in horror as he filled the siphon from the barrel and ran it into her father's best decanter.

She began to be really afraid of him, afraid in a way that she had never been of anyone before or since. Now for the very first time she understood something that had been obvious to both him and the Major—something she had been too proud ever to ask about but was so self-evident that the two men had taken it as not needing explanation—that Henriette was Bálint's child. Relationships depend not on age but on something quite different. And because he had lost his child, the soldier who had come to her house and kissed her with such passion in the doorway was at that moment capable of anything.

He swung round, still holding the siphon. He must have seen something in her face because he smiled. It was not a pleasant smile. She turned her face away: the moment she got back to the house she would have to wake her father, whatever the consequences. He kept on walking, toward the air-raid shelter. When he finally got there he switched the light on, stood the siphon on a table, and looked along the shelf. It was one she had put up herself when they were fitting the place out. He's looking for a glass, she thought: now to leave him there and run. But she couldn't. He grabbed her by the wrist and pulled her down on the bench beside him. He poured a glass of wine for himself, put another in her hand, and drank his in one go. She didn't drink but stayed where she was beside him. Then he turned away and burst into tears.

The shelter had been fitted out by Mr. Elekes and it showed all the signs of his thoughtful execution. On the table was a book of prayers; in the corner a wide range of tools and utensils, including an ax and a spade; flashlights on the shelf; tins of food, an unopened box of biscuits, and a first-aid kit on a ledge next to the faucet; a crucifix on the wall and three sleeping bunks made up with blankets and pillows alongside it. The sight of these humble devices for saving human life finally opened the floodgates to the mortal grief inside him. He started to speak, but his voice was mangled by the pressure of emotion and the only word she could make out was "Henriette." Irén was shocked by how, just a few days earlier, that name had so riven her heart, and that she could have been so jealous of the child. She too burst into tears, and the two of them sat there holding a wake for Henriette. Finally she drank the glass of wine he had poured for her.

They had rarely talked about love. They had loved each other too long for that. To analyze their relationship or theorize about it would have been pointless, like commenting every morning that the sun had risen. Their parents had seen, and known, what was happening between them, had made an assessment of their mutual feelings and realized long before they themselves did where it would end. Even when they made the decision that they would eventually marry without waiting for the war to end before announcing their engagement, Bálint hadn't told Irén that he loved her. When he did propose, it was in his usual everyday same tone. He simply said, between two other observations, "I shall marry you, Irén." The announcement, for which she had been waiting for so many years, had surprised her so little that it failed to strike her that he hadn't expressed it more romantically—or given any reason for declaring himself at that moment. She knew that he loved her. To spell it out would have been superfluous.

Now, for the very first time, he said the words: "Irén, I love you."

She put her glass down, somewhat shocked that in such a sad moment—on the night of Henriette's death—she could experience such an intense feeling of sweet happiness, such guiltless joy. She offered no reply, just sat there and watched him as he drank. She was struck by the urgency of his need. Bálint rarely drank, and then very little. She knew why he was drinking now, with something verging on revulsion at what he was doing, the way you take a bitter medicine. He was drinking for oblivion, for a few minutes of mindless stupor. She turned her head away. Though she loathed the smell of alcohol she had no wish, on that night of nights, to lecture or reproach him. He put his arm around her neck, pulled her toward him, and kissed her again. But she no longer wanted his kisses, not only because his manner was so brutal and he smelled of wine but because the mouth he proffered had suddenly become that of a stranger. She felt again what she had felt earlier when they had sat together weeping for Henriette, that the person beside her was not Bálint but someone else. She struggled to get away from him.

He resisted for a while, then let her go. She stood up at once. She no longer felt safe in the shelter. She wanted to run up the stairs to the garden and get back to the house that way; but he stood up too.

"I love you," he repeated.

She nodded her response: she had heard him the first time. She was now desperate to get outside, but he grabbed her again and barred the way. She was very afraid. He shook her shoulders and looked into her eyes. She had no idea what he saw there, but her fear continued to mount. She tried to break free from his embrace, but he wouldn't let her. She placed her hand on his chest and pushed as hard as she could, but he was stronger than she was, and he pulled her down on the bed.

"I thought you loved me," he said, his voice full of surprise, as if he had missed something, as if there was something he couldn't see that was somehow obvious to her. They were now lying on the bed—it was the one on which her mother slept—with his body half alongside hers. She began to weep; she scratched and fought. He endured it with surprising coolness, trying all the while to remove her clothes with great care, as if wishing to avoid causing her pain while permitting no resistance.

Irén had always wanted to be his, his alone and no one else's. But not like this, not at such a time, not in the air-raid shelter, and certainly not simply because he was filled with grief at the loss of Henriette. It was so evident that she did not want him at that moment that his hand suddenly stopped moving and let her go. Their engagement rings flashed simultaneously in the lamplight. Irén got up and straightened her clothes, gasping for breath.

"Irén Elekes," he said, as one addresses a pupil at school.

"Irén Elekes, daughter of Abel Elekes. Go. Take yourself off. Leave me. I shall amuse myself here on my own. Go to bed like a good little girl."

He turned his back on her, poured himself another full glass, then let it fall. It rolled across the floor, slowly spilling the wine. "A drunk," Irén said to herself. She could take no more. She would have to go and shout it out in a voice to wake the entire household: "There's a drunken soldier on the property, looting the shelter."

She made for the door but stopped before she got there. She had heard Bálint cursing and sobbing once again. She knew he wasn't weeping for her, or even for the two of them, and she ran on up the stairs. At the gate into the garden she bumped into Blanka. Blanka was standing there, with Irén's dressing gown pulled over her nightdress, leaning forward in the attitude of a listener. Amid the fragrant shrubbery she looked like a figure in a painting.

"Why did you leave him?" she asked, so softly that her lips barely moved. "Why have you come up here?"

Irén made no reply. Her little sister's eyes took in the disheveled hair, the state of her clothes, the missing top button.

"What's he doing down there?" she whispered. Irén had the strange feeling that she knew everything that had gone on in the shelter.

"He's drinking and sobbing."

Later she seemed to remember Blanka murmuring, "The poor man." The younger sister pushed her gently aside and, with a movement of her chin, pointed her toward the garden gate.

"Go to bed."

Later on she realized that she was the one who should have gone back down into the cellar and sent Blanka off to bed. But she didn't. Blanka took a deep breath, like someone about to immerse herself in cold water, and went in through the little door. Irén heard her lock it from the inside.

When Irén became Bálint's wife, they didn't wait for night to fall. He took her straight to the bedroom. In the middle of their embrace she suddenly had the feeling that he was in a hurry, that he just wanted to get it over with. Her own feelings weren't much different; she had a vague feeling that it would have been better with Pali. It was a sunny afternoon, around a quarter to three. As soon as she let him go he reached across to the edge of the sofa and, naked as he was, began to read the newspaper.

1952

BÁLINT had been taken prisoner here in Budapest, transported out of the country, and was among the last to return. Compared to most, he returned in a relatively good physical state, having spent his last years of captivity working in a hospital. I knew nothing of what had happened to him: not a single message from him had reached us, though we later discovered he had sent several. After years had passed without news of him, despite other prisoners having long since returned, my parents and Mrs. Temes became convinced that he was no longer alive. I was the only one who still believed he really would come back, I and Blanka. She was always optimistic, and I simply couldn't accept that life would deprive me of something I wanted so very much. For the old people it seemed somehow natural that he should have disappeared, along with everything else. The Biró household no longer existed, the Major had died in the war, and in the years after Bálint had been taken prisoner their house had been expropriated. Mrs. Temes had managed to save a few of his possessions, in two large trunks, by fraudulently claiming that they had belonged to her late husband. In the chaos after the war she too had had to leave the house. Even if Bálint had been there at the time it would have been difficult for him to explain what sort of person his father had been, the people he had helped, and his role in the lives of so many others. His circle of friends, those he had tried to protect but had been unable to save for lack of time, had been killed off one by one. People who hadn't known him personally knew nothing of his work, only that he had died at the front, and by then it was no longer safe even to mention his name.

So the Birós' house was taken over by the state and the furniture distributed among people dispossessed in the bombing. Mrs. Temes moved out and came to live with us—our house had been classified as too large for our needs and we were required to take in a lodger. In fact her arrival made little difference. We didn't think of it as having a stranger in our midst, because indeed she wasn't one. In fact, having her with us proved a great help. Blanka now had a job, in an office in the hospital where Bálint worked. She had secured it through the Major's influence immediately after passing her last exams, half a year before Bálint was taken prisoner. To our surprise she enjoyed the work, even though she typed atrociously, scattered filing cards everywhere and often lost them. Every so often she received commendations when the families of patients wrote to say what a great help she had been with her few words of comfort, her perennial optimism, and her cheerful smile as she told them not to worry because the patients there always got better.

There were now three of us earning a living, and somehow we managed to get by. In the first school in which I worked the atmosphere felt as natural to me as if I had been born there. My father was delighted when it became apparent that I had inherited his gift for passing on knowledge and ideas and that, despite some initial problems due to inexperience, I was proving to be an excellent teacher. I immersed myself in the life of the school, taking to it as a duck takes to water. I was kept very busy, but I didn't mind: I loved the work, and the good thing was it left me little time to spend wondering where Bálint was, what he was doing, when he would come back, and what shape our lives would take thereafter.

I was on my way home after school, late one afternoon in 1949, and turning down by the church into Katalin Street, when I spotted him in the distance, walking along the road. He was carrying a parcel, not by the string it was wrapped in but squeezed under his arm. Having recognized him from the back I began to run. I caught up with him just as he stopped. A woman was asking him something, presumably for news of her husband or son. I literally tore him away from her, though she tagged along with us for a while, seeming unable to understand that he had no news to give her and that the two of us were in some way connected. She danced along beside us, tugging at his sleeve and shouting something, I can't remember what.

We didn't kiss. We just walked on. I clung to his free left arm and gripped his hand, tears streaming down my face. His features never moved. He too was overjoyed, but somehow he managed to be much more self-controlled than I was. He was heading for his old house and wanted me to go there with him, so the first words he heard from me, apart from shouting out his name and a few stammered words, were not "So you've come home; I love you so much" but the revelation that the house was no longer theirs and he would now be living with us. By then we were standing outside his front door. For some minutes he stared at the handle in silence, then turned away and went on with me toward our house.

He could not have hoped for a warmer welcome than the one he received. Mrs. Temes, shrewd, sensible, and reserved as she was, hugged him and kissed him, probably for the first time since he had become a man, and even my mother's childish giggles had something restrained about them. She neither threw herself at him nor swamped him with silly questions or dark tales of disaster. My father's delight was betrayed only by the way he pottered about in silence. I was the least relaxed of all of us, because Bálint was showing the same degree of reserve towards me. When Blanka arrived home from the cinema he tried to lift her off her feet the way he once did, but he failed. He said she weighed a ton, and his muscles weren't what they had been. I stayed aloof from all of this, both embarrassed and on my guard. Whenever I finally got something I had wanted very badly, it always took a while before I could behave naturally again.

Bálint's case passed quickly through the review and normalization process, he returned to his job in the hospital, and life resumed its course. Every morning the four of us would set off to work, Bálint and Blanka to the hospital and my father and I to our respective schools. When we pressed Bálint with questions about his time as a prisoner he simply responded with amusing anecdotes. I never once heard him complain. But the months went by and he still was not his old self. He almost never kissed me, and when he did it was on my hair or my cheek; occasionally he would squeeze my hand or stroke my shoulder—as if a mere gentle touch were sufficient substitute for proper physical contact.

As time went by I found that increasingly unsatisfactory. Once I had gotten over the stress of thinking I would never see him again and had grown used to the fact that he really was back, my body began to crave what it had been so abruptly denied on the evening of Henriette's death. I was now twenty-five and had still not experienced lovemaking. We were living under the same roof, we were officially engaged to each other, and whenever we found ourselves together without other company I kept waiting for him to touch me the way he had on that previous occasion. Instead we lived like brother and sister. He gave most of his salary to my father for his board and lodging, and it was accepted, because even with our own three salaries just getting by was difficult. Had it not been for Mrs. Temes's ingenuity we would have eaten even less well than we did. He lived with us, among us, alongside us, but never once talked of marriage.

I still had my engagement ring, but he no longer had his. Initially I was reluctant to raise the subject, then too embarrassed, and in the end I just didn't dare. I sat and discussed the problem with Blanka, my parents, and Mrs. Temes in an attempt to fathom his behavior. My father took the view that it would be indelicate to sound him out directly, and he forbade Blanka from saying anything to him about it. In the end Mrs. Temes went to speak to him. She returned as soon as their conversation was over, whereupon Bálint immediately left the house, no doubt guessing that we would be picking over what he had told her. He had said that his future in the hospital was uncertain. He was being sidelined and deliberately underemployed, whereas my life was moving in the opposite direction and was clearly on the rise. I had somehow managed to gain acceptance and had landed on my feet, but he had no idea how his own future would turn out—probably he wouldn't have one. He needed to know more about where he stood, and whether he was going to be left alone despite the fact of who his father had been. So we would just have to wait. At the moment he wasn't in a position to resume where we had left off. If this was too much for my father to bear, or if I were to be presented with a better prospect, we should feel free to show him the door and he wouldn't hold it against us.

I couldn't look anyone in the face. I stared down at my lap, as if amazed that I should possess such things as hands and knees. My mother was beside herself, calling him every name under the sun, and Blanka shrieked that he was a coward. My father and Mrs. Temes were more reserved. My father, as a man, probably had a better insight into what Bálint was feeling, while Mrs. Temes made no bones about taking his side. She thought that, as far as it was possible, we should let him be. He was like his father, he had a proud nature, and it must be very hard for him to swallow the fact that rather than taking a wife he was now being taken in as a husband-to-be, and that instead of carrying Irén off to live with him in his father's house, here he was, a mere lodger with her family.

When he finally arrived home that evening, and we had all had supper, I went with him into the garden. He told me, which I already knew, that Mrs. Temes had been putting her nose into our affairs and it was time for us to talk about things, for us to stand together. I told him I was in no hurry (I was in a desperate hurry but I was too proud to say so) and I would wait, if that was what he wanted. And he wasn't to trouble himself about the fact that he was living with us. Things were fine as they were.

He looked at me and placed his hand on my knee. Where now was the soldier who had pressed those burning kisses on me, who had pulled me down beside him on the camp bed that evening in the shelter? He was handling me as if I were a child, a child close to him, a child he loved. I trembled under his touch and waited for him to tell me more than he had Mrs. Temes. He must surely have sensed how unhappy

I was, how humiliated, and that the reasons he had given had not convinced me. Mrs. Temes might understand why he was looking for a way out but I certainly didn't, because now that he was my fiancé he had absolutely nothing to fear. While his fingers lingered on my knee I was ready for everything. I was waiting for him to speak to me the way he had spoken to Henriette that night, to start telling me stories— that as soon as he felt more secure in his place of work he would take me to Salzburg or Rome, and seeing me would make the pope sad because he was not allowed to marry. But he said nothing. More precisely, what he did say left me stunned: "You are such a strong person, Irén, always so sure of everything."

My father had raised me always to face up to things, to stand on my own two feet and not bellow like Blanka or shout and scream like my mother. Bálint did not elaborate on his remarks, but I knew what he was unable to say, what he was holding back: that he, in contrast, was weak and unsure of himself, and that he was for some reason deeply troubled precisely by what I considered the greatest of my virtues. Inside my head I was hearing something I really didn't want to: that in the situation he found himself in, having lost his father and his home, and feeling so insecure in his job, he needed someone rather different, someone who could show him more understanding, someone like Henriette, perhaps. The two of them would have been able to share their doubts and confide their fears to each other—fears both for themselves and of something else as well, something I had no fear of because I didn't know what it was or that it was lying in wait for me too. They would share the same awareness of the dead: she because she was no longer alive, and he because he had seen too much of death and had learned something in the prison camp that I knew nothing of but Henriette did, because she too had been a prisoner, if only briefly, in his father's house.

We sat there in silence, like a well brought up brother and sister. It was the first time in my life that I had an inkling that the dead are not dead but continue living in this world, in one form or another, indestructibly. It occurred to me that if the Helds and the Major and Henriette had still been with us, then one day Bálint would kiss me again the way he had before. On the other hand, if those who had died had taken something fundamental away from him in their dying, then I would probably never be able to give that back to him, not because I didn't love him, or because I wasn't trying hard enough, but because there was no way in which I conceivably could. It was simply impossible.

So there we sat. I had only ever seen the Major's wife in a painting, the one in which she held a tiny Bálint on her lap, being dandled close to her. And here he was, sitting beside me, and I knew I could do nothing more for him than let him lean on my shoulder and offer him a few minutes' support, and that he would want nothing more. I still loved him, even though I had guessed some time before what had been made so clear that evening, both about him and the others. But I still wanted to marry him, even though I knew it would be rather like Lenore's marriage to Wilhelm in the German ballad. Bálint, like Wilhelm, had died in his own Battle of Prague, and if he did ever become mine, I too would have a very strange husband indeed, in a relationship every bit as bizarre, unreal, and terrifying as the girl finds in the legend. He asks her, *Graut's Liebchen auch?* (Are you frightened too, my dear?) No, I wasn't afraid, not at all. I wanted him, even though I knew that it would bring me endless pain and trouble. I felt the same way years later when he told me at the exhibition, without any preamble, that he would marry me—even though by then I was married to Pali, Kinga had been born, and it was a long time since I had last loved him.

In the years that followed my father had good reason to be proud of me. I was promoted to the role of deputy head at an incredibly early age, moving into the top rank of my profession. He felt that all his own thwarted ambitions were being realized in me, and he was happy. My mother understood little of my working life, but her face lit up every time she looked at me, and each time I came home and recounted the day's doings and my triumphs therein she listened with open mouth. She was in fact so happy and so proud of me that she made an effort to be more disciplined herself. Neighbors and colleagues from the school often came to the apartment to talk about things and discuss concerns of mutual interest over a cup of coffee, and when anyone arrived she would rush out of the room to adjust her permanently wrinkled stockings and then make a real effort to say something intelligent. But even if I had been a more outgoing person I would never have been able to share my burden with any of these people. My one confidante was Blanka.

My little sister had often been in love during this period, only to be disillusioned time after time. We all suspected that she was leading a rather freer sort of life than we imagined, but the subject was never mentioned: a chatterbox she might be, but she also knew how to stay silent when she wanted. Her childish boisterousness was now much softened, and when I woke her abruptly from her dreams because I needed to talk about things I had been too ashamed to mention during the day, she always listened attentively and sympathetically. At first she reassured me, saying that one day the lunatic would come to his senses, but as time passed she became less certain and eventually stopped offering these consolations altogether. When my expressions of unhappiness and concern were met only with silence, I realized that something was going on that Bálint wasn't telling me. I continued to wait for an explanation. It took some time, but in the end it came.

It was in 1952. Bálint had been living with us for three years and had never replaced the ring he had lost, though I was still loyally wearing mine. He lived with us and among us like an old-fashioned gentleman lodger. Finally Blanka spoke out. She told me that I would have to confront him and insist that we marry. He was having affairs, not with people who worked at the hospital but with cheap little tarts, the real dregs: all sorts of people went there, and his affairs were with anyone he could pick up. He was living the life of a madman, quite shamelessly, without any attempt at self-control. He needed to pull himself together. In any case, his employment there hung by a thread. He was being moved around all the time, always in a new role. Just then he was working in the same office as she was, so she could see for herself how he spent his time.

I kept faith with Bálint and waited for him patiently. I shed tears but never in front of him. I clung to the idea that it was the curse of his higher social class that stood between us; that the war and his imprisonment had damaged him; that his father, the Major, had been a support to him all his life but in death was now a hindrance . . . but none of that really mattered, nor did it bother me however much he was being kept down in the hospital—no one there had the power to change my feelings for him. I didn't mind if they denied him advancement, if they never gave him the kind of work he deserved, if he remained a nobody. But that he was taking lovers and still didn't want to marry me…that I couldn't bear.

With Blanka shouting after me to stop, I flung on my dressing gown and ran through the dining room where Mrs. Temes was sleeping and on to the study, where Bálint lodged. I turned on the light, accidentally hitting the adjoining switch to the chandelier. It came on as well and the room lit up as if the house were on fire. Bálint was startled awake. He leaped out of bed and stared at me, with everything around, above, and behind him ablaze with light. I yelled at him so loudly that I woke the entire house, but I didn't care if every single one of them gathered to eavesdrop behind the door. I don't remember exactly what I said, but it was along the lines that I knew about his girlfriends; they were the reason he was unwilling to marry me; I'd had quite enough of the sordid life we were leading, but I would overlook everything if we could be married that week. I would put everything to rights and make an end of this humiliating and mindless existence we shared.

I screamed and sobbed. I could scarcely see through my tears. By the time I had managed to pull myself together he had hauled on a dressing gown and was standing before me, staring into my eyes. He had never looked at me that way before. I felt quite sure he had never looked like that at Blanka or Henriette. This was something altogether new.

"Go and find yourself a husband, Irén," he said. "You're a thoroughly nice girl, and everything's going your way. Get married and have children. I'll clear out as soon as I can find somewhere to stay. I've been waiting for you to take that ring off your finger and kick me out. The cruelty you've all shown me, with your endless patience, is appalling. You should have worked out what was happening a long time ago."

I stared at him in amazement. He lit a cigarette. It was the first time I had seen him looking calm and relaxed since he had returned home. He looked happy, his old self, as he had been when we were children or young adults.

"So it'll all turn out very nicely, then," he remarked, and he kissed me. (At last he kisses me!) "You'll have your peace of mind back; everything will be fine. One day we'll even be able to take out passports again and travel. You've never been anywhere. You'll go to places you've always wanted to see. You'll feed the pigeons in St. Mark's Square, you'll visit Naples."

By then I was tugging at my engagement ring. At last I got it off and slapped it down on the table in front of him. By the time I left the room the place had been emptied—even the bed Mrs. Temes had been sleeping in. I reckoned they must all be in the kitchen, sitting around in their pajamas, confused and dismayed. Only Blanka was still there, and then she went off to bed. I didn't cry. I was beyond tears. I sat down beside her and reflected on how cheap he must think me, how very lower middle class. For Henriette it was Salzburg and the pope; for me, Naples—a commonplace wall poster.

"I'll make him pay for this," she said, to my surprise.

I looked at her, but saw only a blur where her face should have been and another where her body was. For the first time since I had come to self-awareness there would be no Bálint in my life, and the thought was so surreal that my senses seemed to have taken on a life of their own. I didn't fully grasp what she had said. She might as well have spoken in a foreign language for all that I could make of it. She was weeping for me, and I was no longer capable of tears.

When, years later, the subject came up between them, Bálint never managed to make Irén understand what a relief the disciplinary hearing had been for him, how it had forced a decision he never could have made on his own. She just stared at him uncomprehendingly, then kissed him. He submitted with some irritation, as if he were being given a reward for something that he hadn't earned. It annoyed him too that he could never make her believe that he wasn't angry with Blanka for the part she had played—and not for any chivalrous reasons either. He wasn't angry with anyone, in fact, not even the senior manager who had presided over the hearing and whom history had since swept away and deposited God knows where. There were things she found it impossible to understand, and the older she became the harder it was for her. At one point, when their marriage was going through a relatively stable period, he had tried to tell her what it had really been like in the prison camp, but she simply blocked her ears and yelled at him that she couldn't bear to hear about his sufferings. That did shock him. His worst experiences were no longer something he dwelt on; he now preferred to focus on quite different things, from both his imprisonment and the four correctional years he had been forced to spend in the country.

The older Irén got the more she became like her father.

She responded to things in an increasingly trite and school-teacherly way. He could tell in advance the exact words in which she would decide what he was going to say even before he had said it: the miserable captive, the starving prisoner, the object of universal vilification. In truth he needed another man to share his prisoner-of-war memories with; no woman would ever grasp the idea that there could be something comforting in captivity and oppression, and that losing the right to arrange your own life at the same time absolved you of responsibility, because if someone else was deciding everything for you, however harshly or stupidly—providing you with food and dictating your hours of work and leisure, in short, treating you not especially badly but simply as a child—it relieved you of what Bálint so hated and feared, exercising his own free will and the need to make his own decisions.

When he was finally released it left him even more confused than when he had first been captured. The thought that he would now have to go home filled him with something like horror—having to face the fact that everything there would have changed, that he would have to take responsibility for himself, be married, and raise children. Naturally he would not have told Irén that while he was a prisoner he had thought about her very little, even though he longed for female company and for lovemaking. The faces of the women he conjured up in his mind rarely resembled hers. When he did think of her, it simply reminded him that certain standards would be expected of him once he was back, a degree of integrity. The very idea made him feel exhausted and not in the least sure he could live up to it.

At the hearing itself, nothing had surprised him—only the charge laid against him and the person making it. He had expected to be hauled up on account of his immoral private life. At least that made some sense, even though he couldn't see what bearing the way he spent his free time had on his medical work. But that question was raised only as a side issue, a form of supporting evidence. When he first saw Blanka in the chamber, he assumed she had been seconded to write the official minutes and he felt rather sorry for her. She was always so flustered and unable to concentrate that she would have to transcribe everything several times. But he was glad to see her there. It was now the fourth week since he had left the Elekeses, and every time he had spoken to her in her office to ask about her family she had looked straight through him and refused to reply; obviously she hadn't been able to forgive him for leaving Irén. But even if she were sulking she still was part of his life, and he would have liked to reassure her that they all mattered to him just as much as ever, and that the situation wasn't as they seemed to imagine but really much simpler. What he had learned about himself during his time as a prisoner, and about his new circumstances following his release, had been so over-whelming that he had no desire to burden Irén with it, and neither did he wish to burden himself with her problems.

The presiding officer ordered him to sit in silence while the charge was read out. He lit a cigarette and listened to the long list of nurses, junior doctors, and former patients with whom he'd had relationships over the past few years. If he felt at all anxious it was for the women involved. He hoped that they wouldn't find themselves in trouble because of him; if anyone was to blame he was. But when he heard the name of his accuser, and her reasons, he burst into laughter. She had been avoiding his gaze; now she looked at him for the first time.

Blanka had always had difficulty expressing herself, and once again she stammered and spluttered and struggled to get to the point. It eventually emerged that she was accusing him of taking bribes from his patients. She had seen this happen many times, she claimed, because Bálint had worked with her in admissions. On the last occasion it had been a Mrs. Iméréne Karr. Mrs. Karr had been given instant admission into a small side ward after slipping an envelope into his hand. Bálint had made no promises before he opened the envelope, but had said he would see what he could do, and the result was that the woman was immediately put in a bed next to the window in a comfortable room for four people where, most unusually, she was the sole occupant.

Blanka stammered and blushed. Bálint watched her, with her brave little gun, her plump little body stuffed into those odd-looking trousers and doublet, her hair that had defied Mrs. Held's curling iron, and the cardboard helmet. Throughout the hearing he saw her sitting there in her costume, and Henriette, who happened to be in the neighborhood and had come to look for them, was baffled as to why she could see Blanka sitting there in the hospital in fancy dress and Bálint in his Hussar costume of old. Her sense of surprise soon faded, though, because every time she went home she found things that were more and more incredible—Mr. Elekes half blind and writing little plays about the victims of fascism; Mrs. Temes having moved in with them and resenting her loss of independence; Mrs. Elekes prattling away about problems of socialist education with Irén's fellow teachers; Irén herself, an unhappy, hard-faced Irén who had not been married; and the balding, womanizing Bálint—they all seemed as improbable to her as if they were at a fancy-dress ball or had been cast in unsuitable parts in a not very good play. Well, if that was what they wanted, why should he not wear his Hussar's uniform and she carry her rifle, and they both enjoy themselves?

Bálint remembered Mrs. Karr. She had arrived at the hospital a good fortnight earlier and had indeed asked to be placed in a side ward because she hated being with lots of other people. She was a plump, smiling woman who had come unaccompanied on a referral by her local doctor and presenting unmistakable symptoms of appendicitis. He had declined to respond to her request, had admitted her and told her that the people in the ward would decide where to place her, as it always depended on what beds were available at the time; he immediately turned to the next patient in the queue and Mrs. Karr moved on. Blanka was sitting nearby typing, as usual. If anyone could have overheard the conversation it was she. The revelation that she was the one trying to destroy his career left him more amused than shocked.

He realized too why she had chosen Mrs. Karr. She had died soon after the operation, one of those inexplicable deaths that sometimes follow appendicitis. The case was looked into, her relatives took her things away, and because there were so many other patients to deal with, Bálint had more or less forgotten her.

Blanka was looking him straight in the eye, and while she stammered and stuttered out her speech, her little gun seemed to be leveled at him too. Not one word of the accusation was true, but there was no one but Mrs. Karr who could have refuted it: she had deliberately chosen a patient who was now dead. It meant that the charge was probably enough, along with everything else—all the other irregularities in his way of life—to have him dismissed. Blanka rounded off her speech with a few ill-formulated sanctimonious pseudo-socialist platitudes, drawing the panel's attention to the need for vigilance in the maintenance of medical ethics. Only then did Bálint remember the phrase he had been trying to recover since the start of the proceedings—Blanka's line in the play. To everyone's astonishment he declaimed: "I shall attack you, I shall vanquish you, I shall chop your arms and legs to pieces." The party official thought he had gone mad. Then he also remembered the way he had wrestled with Blanka on the stage until Mr. Elekes had come to his aid, and how strong she had been, how unusually strong and brave for a girl.... Finally Blanka sat down and lowered her rifle.

In his reply he found himself calmer and more composed than he had expected. Neither the director who was presiding, the party official, nor the four members of the panel could have suspected how happy he was to be leaving the hospital his father had intended him for ever since he had been a schoolboy, and where since his return from captivity he had been given only the most unrewarding tasks. He denied the charge of having taken a bribe from the patient. Of course he couldn't prove it, but neither could Blanka prove the opposite. He suspected that this issue would be at the center of their deliberations, and the decision would rest on which of the two of them was believed. There was only one assertion that Blanka could back up: that the two of them had been the only people present in the five minutes it took to admit Mrs. Karr, since their two colleagues had gone out, one for lunch and the other to the toilet.

They were asked to leave the room while the panel considered their decision. Before Blanka could slip away into her office, Bálint seized her by the arm. Once again he sensed how strong she was and how fiercely she resisted, but he quickly overpowered her and pulled her into an embrace. She writhed and twisted in his arms but was unable to free herself. They hadn't spoken to each other since he had left the house and he really hoped she would listen to him now. Instead she uttered a piercing scream. The door opened and the presiding director looked out. Bálint was obliged to let her go. "Now they'll think I was trying to strangle her," he told himself, and she ran off down the corridor. He was no longer seeing her in her military breeches but in a little girl's dress, dark blue—Irén had told her that dark blue was always appropriate, especially for a disciplinary hearing. No one would understand how dear Blanka was to him, despite her recent testimony and the fact that he was well aware of her little tricks and her foul temper. What a hope! The official who looked out of that door when she screamed would have seen him as a serial offender. If there had been any doubt remaining as to the outcome, the truth was now clear. He had been harassing the poor girl, or trying to persuade her through physical intimacy to withdraw her allegations.

When they finally called him in he was told that he would be transferred out of the hospital for disciplinary reasons. The ministry had chosen a village where there was no electric lighting but where improvements would be made under the next five-year plan. The ministry representative gave him another hard look, and Bálint wondered if he was trying to see what women found so attractive in him—so pale and thin, a real nonentity. Throughout the hearing, apart from the mention of Mrs. Karr's envelope, there had been references to his womanizing. It was clearly so painful to hear that one member of the panel, a female doctor, had stared determinedly at the floor all the while. He had felt quite sorry for her; she'd had to endure a list of such Leporello-like proportions that she must finally have realized why he hadn't bedded her too. Much as the poor fellow had wanted to, he simply hadn't had the time.

The recommendation was that he should mend his ways, practice self-criticism, and be very grateful that he was being allowed to continue earning his living. He was then dismissed. He went out, delighted beyond words by the knowledge that he would be entitled to government accommodation in the village where they were posting him. To date he had been living first as a gentleman lodger and husband-to-be with the Elekes family and then, in circumstances that defied description, in a rented room in a tiny side street off the Inner Ring Road. "Principal and sole tenant," he reflected delightedly, and then felt surprised that he could still take pleasure in something. "Blanka, what a pumpkin head, you poor little thing!"

He was on his way to the admissions office to collect his belongings when he heard someone behind him—the sound of hurrying footsteps. It was one of the members of the panel, a colleague. He was just a casual acquaintance, someone he exchanged greetings with, who worked in another part of the hospital, and his name was Timár. Bálint stopped, wondering what the man wanted. He obviously wanted something.

Timár told him he didn't believe a single word of the charges made against him, and he wasn't the only one. It was only those who had been trained to accept whatever they were told. It was all because of who his father had been and that sleazy little trollop who had brought the charges, no doubt in revenge because she hadn't made it with him. But one day he would be back in his place in the hospital, and he should remember that it was he, Timár, who had told him so. He shook Bálint's hand and disappeared.

The man's words made little impression on him, nor was he very interested. In fact he was rather irritated by what he had heard. The man should have spoken out at the time, but he just sat there in silence, and now he had come to offer his condolences. Why bother? And why did he call Blanka—his little soldier with her rifle—a trollop? And anyway the bit about his womanizing was all true, though it didn't stop him being a good doctor. It was all nonsense.

He found Blanka in the office, huddled over her typewriter, her back to the door. The two other employees stood up to greet him as he came in. They had never done so before. "So now I'm a martyr," he said to himself. He smiled briefly and began to empty his desk drawers. Henriette, who was now standing beside him, watched as he packed up his belongings and reflected how strange it was that he should have so many lovers—and that he had never kissed her *that way*. It surprised her to realize that it still hurt her, and that a pain felt in her previous life should so linger on. Once he had gathered his personal belongings—there weren't very many of them, just enough to fill his briefcase—Bálint was debating whether to say goodbye to the girls, when they solved the problem for him by coming forward and shaking his hand. Blanka stayed in her chair and said nothing.

He was already outside, in the hospital park, when he remembered his coat: he had taken it off when he went to the director's office. He felt reluctant to go back, but eventually decided to do so after all. It was one of the things that Mrs. Temes had rescued from his former home. He had found it in the trunk in the Elekeses' house.

Going back into the office again, he noticed that everything had been moved around. Previously Blanka's desk had been between the two other girls'; it had now been dragged into a corner. She was standing beside it, in tears, her faced buried in her hands. The two other girls, with all the solemnity of priestesses, were setting out their things on the other two tables, which were now side by side. There was a wide gap between their desks and Blanka's. "My God," Bálint thought. "She's being ostracized as an informer and a traitor."

He had so many memories of that face...howling with anguish and chuckling with laughter, riding on a sleigh, terrified of the visiting chimney sweep, cramming for her exams, and crying...and also the sheer joy of her, the Blanka who had yielded to his embraces on Mrs. Elekes's camp bed in the shelter...and there she was again, with her little gun, now dancing around, now as a fully grown girl, in a real woman's dress...and again he wanted to caress her. He moved toward her, but the older of the office workers, the more serious-looking, stepped in between them. "No," she said sternly. "Not even God would go that far. Don't. She doesn't deserve it." She took his white coat down from its hook, folded it, and handed it to him. He had to carry it over his arm as his briefcase was full.

He left the room feeling miserable and tense—not because of what had happened earlier but because he had been unable to say goodbye to Blanka. "It's 1952," Henriette was thinking, as she followed Bálint out. For a moment she wondered whether she shouldn't perhaps stay with Blanka, whose actions and attitude had completely baffled her. "What's going on between them? What's this all about? If I were still alive I'd be twenty-four by now."

IT HAD been about three months since Bálint had moved out, and by then I could bear his absence no longer. Let him do what he liked, run after women if he wanted to, he simply had to come back and live with us. He was one of us, part of our lives. He didn't have to marry me if he didn't want to but at least we would be able to talk sometimes. I no longer had my pride, and after everything that had happened the thought of having to say all this to him no longer filled me with dread. I didn't know his new address, and when I asked Blanka to give him a message at the hospital to suggest a time and place for us to meet, she told me that she wouldn't even if he were still there, but anyway he was no longer in town: he had been transferred out.

I thought she must be teasing me, or even lying, not wanting to be the person responsible for bringing him back. But she wasn't teasing. Then, to my surprise, she became really angry with me and, for the first time ever in our lives, began to lecture me: what sort of person was I to want him back after all he had done to humiliate me? Blazing with passion, she told me what a wonderful person I was and what a nobody he was, and what a prize he had let slip through his hands once I had accepted him. "Just drop it," I shouted, and stared at her as if she were talking in a fever or had simply gone mad. I just couldn't believe that Bálint wasn't in Budapest.

I thought it was a lie to stop me asking him to come back. I could have hit her for being so contemptible, so brazen, and for refusing to help even though she knew how much Bálint meant to me.

I didn't dare ask my father to intervene. There would have been no point. Being even prouder than I was he had been even more offended by Bálint's departure. Mrs. Temes was so ashamed of the way he had behaved—a boy she had raised herself—that I didn't want to involve her either. I didn't know who to turn to, apart from my mother. She was both alarmed and exalted by the fact that for the first time in my life I was now asking for her help, sobbing in her bedroom and begging her to put an end to everything that had gone wrong. There was an unwritten rule in the family that she was a sort of junior member, someone who knew little of the world and had to be sheltered from it. But that I was suffering she did understand. She agreed to try and find out if Blanka was telling the truth, or rather what it was that she was holding back. I have never since seen her the way she looked as she set forth, having tidied her coat and her shoes and done her hair, twice.

It was the fifth of December and the snow had already arrived. I stood by the window looking out into the garden, though there was nothing to be seen in the late-afternoon gloom. Blanka was out. She often stayed out long after she had finished work, but she hadn't introduced us to any new boyfriends for a while and we had no idea where she went or who she was with.

Mrs. Temes was busy in the kitchen, preparing the meal for St. Nicholas Eve. My father noticed that I had finished my work and told me to put the traditional shoes in the window. My mother still wasn't home. He had no idea where she was, as she had gone out before he returned. I stammered something about her having gone to visit someone—a silly suggestion that he clearly didn't believe. A little later Mrs. Temes joined us in the sitting room, with her sewing things. She too expressed wonder about where my mother could possibly be.

Eventually Blanka arrived. She smelled of alcohol. There was a glint in her eye, something in her manner, some suggestion that she had been out having a good time with a man, someone rather special to her. She was in high spirits, almost triumphant.

At last my mother was back. Of course she had forgotten to take her key—she was always forgetting to take it—and had to ring the bell. I was so desperate to hear what she had to say, so full of hopes and fears, that I was incapable of speech. She seemed almost childlike that evening, apprehensive, as if afraid of something. I had never seen her quite like that before. I guessed at once that Bálint wasn't in Budapest and that things were much more serious than I had thought. As soon as she stepped inside she was bombarded with questions about where she had been, but she made no reply and simply threw down her coat. My father waited a while to see if either Blanka or I would get up, and then, since nobody else was going to, rose to his feet and went to hang it up himself.

Blanka was smoking a cigarette and fiddling about with the radio. She was saying that I ought to go to the hospital for the turning on of the Christmas tree lights; there would be plenty of young unmarried doctors there. She meant well, but it was such a clumsy gesture that I just shook my head. Then it was Mrs. Temes's turn to quiz my mother about where she had been. The next thing we heard was her bursting into tears.

It was only then that we all realized we had not once heard her cry since we learned that the Major had been killed. We instantly gathered round her, and I thought, "He's dead." Her reaction could mean nothing else—she had been too frightened to tell us. I tried to imagine what life would be like without Bálint, but I couldn't. I stood next to her, longing for her to take me in her arms. I never really felt that she was my mother. It was only when I was in distress and on rare occasions like this when she rose above her usual self. I waited for her to draw me to her and caress me. Instead I watched as she pulled Blanka to her. I stared at the two of them in astonishment, almost like an idiot. I was the abandoned fiancée, the one cast aside, effectively Bálint's widow, and it was Blanka she had pulled over and embraced and kissed. It was as if this unprovoked gesture was a way of telling her something that no one yet understood, least of all Blanka herself.

"What's going on here?" my father asked, anxiously. "What happened to you? Where did you go?"

My mother didn't answer. She just went on hugging and kissing Blanka, and then, as if in a sudden fit of madness, started to pummel her. Blanka screamed, tore herself from our mother's grasp, and ran to the window. My mother's weeping took on an edge of grieving, like that of a mourner at a funeral.

I was now desperate for someone to say something, to tell me at last what they knew, to put an end to all this; whatever it was, even if he were dead, even if he had killed himself, I had to know. If my role now was to mourn for him, I was ready for it. I absolutely needed to know, to put an end to this uncertainty in which I swung between wildly conflicting feelings. Mrs. Temes gave my mother something to drink, treating her with the detached solicitude she showed to all of us when we were ill. Gradually my mother pulled herself together, dabbed her face, and became her usual self. She claimed she had been to her dressmaker to order a dress. No one believed her. We all knew she hated buying clothes; she liked only what was old and comfortable, and she had always been too lazy to go and try anything on.

My father made a gesture of resignation. She often told lies, and even if we still had no idea where she had been on that chilly afternoon and why she had attacked Blanka, we were all familiar with the sort of scene we had just witnessed—and at least she had calmed down. The important thing was that she was back home. Sooner or later she would tell us where she had been and what had so upset her. She had never been able to keep a secret.

Mrs. Temes went out to the laundry room. Blanka stayed sulking for a minute, then went over to kiss my mother and got herself ready to go out again, saying that she had to go somewhere, that there were some friends waiting for her. My father said no, she would have to stay at home and do some reading or mend her underwear. It was still St. Nicholas Eve in our house and there was no question that she would be spending it with us. She flounced off to our shared bedroom and my mother went into hers. I followed her in, and at last the two of us were alone. Seeing me, she burst into tears again, but eventually she spoke, dabbing her handkerchief to her eyes all the while, to avoid meeting mine.

Because she hadn't known Bálint's new address she had gone to the hospital to make inquiries. The porter had told her that he no longer worked there and that he had been sent away. She went from one office to another trying to find someone who could tell her more. Finally she spoke to the director, who was just coming out of a meeting. He praised Blanka warmly, describing her as rather flighty but capable of making real progress. She retained none of her bourgeois attitudes: if she saw something wrong anywhere she would try to put it right, even if it cost her something because of her upbringing and her present connections. My mother had no idea what he was referring to, so he spelled out in simpler language what had happened to Bálint, making it clear that Blanka was the one who had drawn the hospital's attention to the need to get rid of him.

I just couldn't take in what she was telling me. It was all perfectly straightforward and even now I have no idea why it was so difficult for me, why I had to make her tell the story over and over again before I could understand what my sister had done. When the penny finally dropped, I had to sit down. Up to that point I had refused to believe that what there was between Bálint and me could ever come to an end. Slamming my ring down in front of him had been pointless. I had thought it was just a question of time and all would be well again. Now there was no longer any reason to hope. Not ever.

In such moments of crisis, when our troubles become too much to bear, often quite trivial things take on significance. My brain ceased to function, and all I could think of now was how I could possibly continue to share a bedroom with Blanka after what had happened.

Well, I wasn't forced to carry on sharing that bedroom. I had made myself ready to go out and was just about to leave when I found my father standing behind me in the entrance hall. He had obviously been there for some time. In his hand was the red crepe-paper-covered St. Nicholas bell that he always rang in their bedroom. Thinking about what my mother had told us had brought him to a halt while still in the entrance hall. He was holding the bell by its clapper to stop it ringing—to prevent it ringing in the festival in our house. I went and stood beside him. He said nothing, then followed me into his study.

Again I was forced to sit down. My legs could no longer support me. My father left me there and carried on into the shared bedroom, still clutching the St. Nicholas bell. He was there for ages. I heard only his voice speaking: Blanka said nothing in reply. When he came back his face was no longer pale, it was bright red. He sat down beneath the bust of Cicero and placed his book in front of him. My mother came out of their bedroom and—something I had never seen before—sat down beside him at the desk. At that moment it didn't seem at all odd, even though I had never known anyone who had less to do with desks and books than her. They sat there like twins, one plunged in grief and the other consumed by shame. Neither said anything to me, or to each other, and neither of them made any effort to comfort me.

Blanka came out of the bedroom, wearing her coat and a head scarf and carrying a suitcase. I went up to her, stared in her face, my eyes blazing, and demanded to know what she had done. She made no reply. She simply touched my arm, very gently, not the often rather forceful push that I was used to, and went over to my father. He didn't look up from his book. She just stood there, waiting for him to come to the end of his page. My mother's gaze went from Blanka to me and from me to Blanka, her head moving from side to side like a terrified doll. Finally she made up her mind. She stood up, hugged Blanka, whispered something in her ear, then followed her as she started to leave the room. Blanka left the house without having spoken once. All we could hear was my mother sobbing. She didn't come back to join us. She went straight to her bedroom and shut the door behind her.

I collapsed on the sofa. In my lessons I like to teach children about the old heroes, and I think I do it rather well. My lessons are enjoyable, and I believe I have a special feel for bringing out the human element in moments of greatness. Even as a child I was enthralled by the idea of destiny and those tragic situations in which morality proves triumphant. Now, seeing my father sitting there under his bust of Cicero, I was struck by two things quite unconnected with my present sufferings. One of them I should have realized long before. I had always believed that I had been my father's favorite, the apple of his eye. Now it was as if he were telling me that it wasn't just my mother who loved my sister more than she loved me; he did too. I cannot think why. Perhaps there was more to forgive in her case, perhaps because she was less like him than I was, or because she was so lacking in independence, so scatterbrained and silly—God knows. Whatever love we receive always comes as a form of grace.

The other thing I realized was that in driving Blanka out of the house he was abandoning her to a deeply uncertain future, but one whose outcome, given her idleness and fecklessness, left no doubt. In denouncing Bálint, and above all in defaming him—the Bálint we had known since childhood, and whom she had been better placed than anyone to know that he would never accept money in this way—she had attacked the entire moral order in which my father believed, and he had acted like the old Hungarian hero Dobozy, who in killing his wife had also killed himself.

Mrs. Temes returned from the laundry room. I stayed where I was because I couldn't bear going back into the empty bedroom, and I hadn't the courage to go and see what Blanka would have taken with her or what she had left. I seemed to be floating, wrenched free from the laws of gravity, having lost my center of balance in this new world, first without Bálint and now without Blanka, the world that the Major and the Helds had already left behind. Mrs. Temes was setting out the festive table. The wall clock was striking the hour of nine. We sat and watched it all the way to the end.

"Well, has St. Nicholas been yet?" Mrs. Temes asked.

The festival was one that had brought all three families together in our house, just as we all went to the Helds for the New Year and to Bálint's house for Easter.

My father stood up. He had forgotten the bell in our bedroom and went to get it. It was from there that we heard it ring as he shook it. Unaware of what had just happened, Mrs. Temes was standing there contentedly. My mother emerged from her bedroom, still dabbing her eyes with her handkerchief. The privilege of opening the window through which St. Nicholas delivered his presents always fell to the youngest, Henriette while she was still alive and now Blanka. Mrs. Temes went and stood at the door of our bedroom, waiting for her to emerge. But only my father appeared. He drew back the curtain and opened the inner window. Outside it was freezing, and we felt the chill of winter instantly penetrate the heated room. In each of the five pairs of shoes was a red parcel. My father took his and started to untie it. His hands were shaking.

"What about Blanka?" asked Mrs. Temes. "Is she asleep?"

"She's gone," my father replied, as he pulled away the silver paper that covered the little figurine made of chocolate. My mother, glutton as she was, just stood there, not touching the sweets. Mrs. Temes looked from one to the other in total incomprehension.

Until 1944 my father had been living in a dream world, from which he began to awaken after the deportation of the Helds, and Henriette's murder had finally established his place as a mere observer. He remained what he always had been, but now more vigilant, more politically aware. He told Mrs. Temes about Blanka, explaining why he was unwilling to sleep under the same roof as an executioner, and it was as if he were talking about someone who was already dead. At that moment Bálint was with us, whether or not he were in the village whose name my mother had instantly forgotten in the hospital; but it was no longer the Bálint we had known of old, Bálint as he had really been. He was simply the victim of an injustice done him by a member of our family, a man who had been condemned by something Blanka had done. Mrs. Temes was not a sentimental woman. She managed to control her feelings. But she could find nothing to say to soften the dry narrative, the sheer brutality, of what my father had said.

My father handed out the presents. On the windowsill one brightly polished shoe remained, with a packet of sweets peeping out. Nobody touched it. Outside, the snow fell steadily.

1956

IN THE car he barely spoke. Cigarette in hand, he watched the wagons laden with food supplies going towards Budapest, with their huge, shy, weary-looking horses that looked so out of keeping in the modern world as they trotted along the highway, shaking their heads as if in wonder at what connection they might have with human affairs.

It simply amazed him how many people, and which people, were making it their business to get him started on a new life. Chief among them was Timár. It was from his mouth that Bálint first heard about the plans to rehabilitate him, and the excited tone in which he spoke struck him as almost comical. He hadn't "suffered" during these last few years, and he felt in no way punished or humiliated by the life that Timár was determined to rescue him from. The village had been overjoyed to have their own doctor at last; they had treated him with respect and showed appreciation for what he did for his patients. It regularly astonished him how little they cared about what had led to his arrival, while those who knew the circumstances of his transfer instantly concluded that he had been the victim of political persecution. He was treated almost like a village pet.

Had Bálint not been concerned about Blanka, Timár would never have succeeded in persuading him to go back even for a few days to accept the compensation the hospital was offering him in person. It was only when he triumphantly mentioned that the old director had now gone, as had almost everyone who had been part of that disciplinary panel, and that only the little trollop who had victimized him was left, and she too would be getting her comeuppance pretty soon, that Bálint threw a few things in his briefcase and got in the car beside him. The gangling youth that Timár had brought either to fill in for him while he was in the capital, or to take his place if he chose to remain there, gazed after the departing car with an expression close to envy.

Bálint's plan was to sort out the situation with Blanka and then go straight back. He had felt wonderful out there in the peace and quiet, where he had at last been able to think calmly about all that had happened in a way that hadn't been possible before. He was therefore somewhat surprised by the feelings that assailed him at the first sight of Budapest.

As the car raced across the first bridge he was astonished at the joy he felt on seeing the city of his birth again, and how a glimpse of the river filled him with such childlike happiness. He was thinking about the different kinds of work he might be doing in the hospital, and looking forward with a certain amount of amusement to the official proceedings, where they would seek to prove beyond doubt what they had been unable to four years before, since Mrs. Karr was still a witness who couldn't be summoned and there was nothing they could do about that. In fact it proved very straightforward. A hearing had taken place a few days earlier and Timár, as the new director, simply presented him with their decision, followed by a few words at a reception immediately afterwards at which his new colleagues were present. People spoke of his many fine qualities and conscientious work, and stated that even before the libelous allegations of

Miss Blanka Elekes he had been subjected to unwarranted persecution because of his class origins. It left him feeling very uncomfortable. In fact the ceremony was rather more painful for him than being arraigned by Blanka.

Timár, acting now in his official capacity, then repeated the invitation for him to return to his old place of work. He promised him an apartment, in due course, naturally; in the meantime he would be accommodated in the hospital itself. He was also offered a new role, one so important that it was obviously being offered in compensation. It should have made him rather more grateful than he felt, but he grew increasingly irritated and restless. However he had no wish to spoil the little homecoming celebration, especially as Timár was so radiant with satisfaction, and he asked for a few days to think things over. He dined with his new colleagues, in a special room where the food was set down before him as if he were the risen Christ. Over the meal he tried to gather some precise details about what lay ahead for Blanka. Timár said she would be summoned before the disciplinary committee, and he added a word about her accusation. "You were just the first," he said indignantly. "She denounced anyone she had a difference with, but she wasn't so clever the next time and the people she accused managed to clear themselves." Along with his official rehabilitation Bálint was awarded a significant sum by way of compensation. He had no idea what he would do with it. That these people had decided to have him back was something he could take no more seriously than that they had wanted to kick him out in the first place.

He made no attempt to look for Blanka in her office. He knew he wouldn't find her there. Whenever she sensed she was in trouble, Blanka's instinct was to run away and hide.

But where could she possibly be? Mrs. Temes had written to him from time to time, and told him as soon as it happened that Mr. Elekes had driven her from the house, that they were not in touch with her and she didn't know her new address. Mrs. Temes was obviously still so angry with Blanka that she hadn't the least interest in what happened to her. Besides she herself was no longer living with the Elekeses. In the same year that Irén got married she had accepted a place in a student hostel, in charge of the kitchen.

Bálint went to see her first. He found her alone in the huge building, public events having drawn the students onto the streets. He asked her if she wasn't worried too. She returned a look of utter incomprehension, as if she had no idea that there might be anything to be concerned about. Her response made him realize just how much she had changed. She showed no pleasure at the news of his rehabilitation and clearly had no conception of what it meant. When he first arrived it had taken some time for her to recognize him. She had shown no particular emotion or joy and had been absentminded, listless, and visibly nervous. Bálint was very fond of Mrs. Temes. He had always viewed her somewhat irregular situation through the eyes of a man rather than a boy, even after he became aware that her relationship with his father went beyond her status of distant relation–cum–housekeeper. Now, as he sat beside her, he felt let down. He wasn't sure what he had expected from her, but it was certainly rather more than he got. He didn't stay with her long. Instead he went on to the Elekeses. As they parted Mrs. Temes told him that she had difficulty sleeping and her digestion was giving her concern, but there was no invitation to call on her again after he had finished whatever he had to do.

He did meet one former acquaintance, and it amused him

to think who it was. The man was a dentist, a fellow captive from the war, someone he hadn't seen since his release. They had made an agreement to look each other up once their old lives resumed, but he hadn't taken it seriously. Both being in the medical line, they had worked in the same hospital in the prison camp, but the man had done rather better out of his time there than Bálint had, not only because he was a lot more streetwise but because he was more outgoing, quicker to make friends, and generally more sanguine. Whenever Bálint thought about him it was with a certain envy. Even in the most grave and troubled situations, Szegi would always come up with some scheme or other, which, with his incredible optimism, he invariably managed to pull off by some inscrutable means. Now, he told Bálint, he was setting off in the morning to see the great wide world—he made it sound as if he were nipping round to the market—and he asked Bálint if he had enough money to pay for the driver to take him to the border too. They were going to Austria. If Bálint had the cash, would he like to go with him? There was still a place on the truck that was leaving. Bálint laughed his refusal. Szegi brushed it aside. In the prison camp he had never been able to understand why Bálint declined to take part in one or another of his schemes. He planned them to perfection and they invariably came off, but they required Bálint to make a decision one way or the other. When it was up to him, Bálint never could make a decision. All the same, Szegi pressed a telephone number into his hand. He could be reached there in the afternoon. If Bálint changed his mind they would come for him in the truck at dawn. They would certainly get out, no worries: he should just trust him. All it needed was the money. Bálint didn't doubt it. Szegi always pulled his little schemes off, but never gratis.

Mrs. Temes's letters had become increasingly confused and downcast, but she had made it clear that he would do well to avoid Katalin Street itself. The old Elekes house was being transformed, along with the Helds' and his own. He had no wish to see how much was being changed, so he made his way to the Elekeses' new abode. Whenever he saw people gathering to form a crowd he kept out of the way and turned down a side street.

The building where Irén and her family now lived was a smart, spanking-new monstrosity. Pressing the bell gave him no sense of unease or embarrassment, despite the fact that he hadn't seen them since Irén had returned his engagement ring. Mr. Elekes opened the door, squinted at him, blinked his eyes for a moment, then gave him a hug and kissed him. Mrs. Elekes clung to his neck shrieking. Neither Irén nor her husband were at home. Irén, they said, was still at school, and her husband, an engineer with the water board, was never back by that time. Mrs. Elekes thrust Irén's little girl into his arms. Kinga showed no fear of him, she just laughed, and Bálint laughed back at her. She was a pretty little thing. If she took after anyone it must be her father—she didn't look like either of the old people or their daughters. But he felt no stirrings of regret that he had not been her father.

The apartment was arranged in much the same way as the old house, though with less furniture, and much of it in a more modern style. Cicero presided, where he always had, above the bookcase behind the desk. Bálint noticed that they had tried to put their larger pieces into the same places they had occupied in the much larger premises in Katalin Street. Sounds of unrest could be heard coming from the city center, and somewhere in the distance there was singing and cheering. He came straight to the point. He wanted

Blanka's address. He needed to speak to her as soon as possible; it was most important.

A heavy silence descended. Mr. Elekes, who had changed very little apart from the strangely distant look in his eyes and the fact that his body seemed to be stiffening and drying out, as if slowly turning to stone, said that he knew nothing about Blanka: they had not been in contact since she had left home. Mrs. Elekes stammered in embarrassment that he really should try to forgive her; she wasn't really such a wicked girl. Bálint started to explain that he had no wish to harm her, he simply wanted to help. He had seen, from the look of terror in their faces, that they were convinced he wanted to call on her for no other reason than to recriminate. But they were also starting to realize that events outside might well take a sudden turn, and that would make it even more important to find out who else their daughter had accused and when. It was no longer a simple question of her ethical conduct but of her safety. Mr. Elekes suddenly remembered that there was a bottle of something rather good in the larder, something Bálint had always enjoyed, and went off to get it. Mrs. Elekes took the opportunity to whisper the address in his ear. She went to see her whenever she could, and added that Irén and her husband also did from time to time: in fact Irén had kept in touch with Blanka ever since her marriage. She gazed anxiously into his eyes, and he assured her once again that she needn't worry; he had never been the least bit angry with Blanka.

Mr. Elekes returned with the apricot brandy. Bálint quickly drank what he had been offered and set out for the city. It was now dark. In every window the shutters were closed, as in wartime. He came across bands of armed men, but they ignored him and just ran past. He tried to think what he would say if they spoke to him, and whether he would actually join them if they asked him to.

Blanka's apartment was in one of those little old streets in the city center. The concierge he spoke to said that as far as she knew she hadn't left the building, but it took him a while to get in. For several minutes he rapped on the grubby knocker, at first despairingly, then with increasing anxiety. Finally he heard someone moving cautiously towards the door and opening the peephole. Blanka's eye peered through it, but only for a moment, and the window was closed again. He shouted to her to open the door.

There was an unnatural, deafening silence inside. Nothing moved. He rang again and kept hammering on the door. As he had so often in the past, he felt like giving her a good smack once he got inside for wasting his time. It was enough to drive one mad. He knew perfectly well that she was in there, just out of reach, doing what she had done all her life when she was afraid—hiding in the bathroom or the larder, assuming there were a larder in such a tiny modern apartment.

However, while Blanka invariably slammed doors, she seldom locked them. They had often teased her about it in the old days. She was always expecting some disaster to happen—a fire, burglars, the Day of Judgment—when she would have to escape at a moment's notice with no time to fiddle with the key. He paused and looked around. She had already put out the rubbish, and next to the doormat there was a bin with a dead cactus on top. It was so typical of her! All her pot plants, everything she laid hands on, withered away: she either overwatered or completely forgot to. He picked up the earthenware pot and smashed the glass in the door. The splinters showered inward. He widened the hole and pressed down on the handle. It was just as he had thought: the door hadn't been locked. He was free to go in. He found her in the second room, squatting low behind the cleaning utensils and various indeterminate boxes. As she had always done as a child when she was afraid, she had her hands pressed over her ears.

He seized her by the arm and dragged her into the bedroom. She must have been hiding in terror for some days now, because everything was perfectly tidy. Whenever she was afraid she tidied things up—emptying a drawer always calmed her down. At this point her terror was so great that the tears were pouring soundlessly from her eyes. He pulled her to him and kissed her. It felt quite strange. He had only embraced her once before in his life, but the intensity and unreality of those fifteen minutes flooded back to him, no less intense and unreal now, if for quite different reasons. He didn't hug her for long. Soon he was holding her the way he had held Irén's child.

Finally she began to realize that he wished her no harm and nestled into his embrace. He told her why he had come, and promised to stay beside her until the hearing, where he would explain to the committee what lay behind her accusation, that it was just something between them, or rather between himself and the Elekes family, a personal hostility, nothing political. He also told her what he had heard from Timár, the news that had so shocked him at the dinner; but he really couldn't believe what they had accused her of. It was all so obviously lies.

"They aren't lying," she said. Her eyes were closed and she was now leaning against his shoulder. "I also accused the girls in the office. Both of them."

He held her away from him so that he could look into her

face. She submitted but refused to open her eyes. She spoke as if in a dream.

"It was because they hated me, they were afraid of me. I was angry with them because they didn't like me."

Her voice was a whisper, as if she were speaking neither to Bálint nor about herself. He listened to her the way he had to her follies and delinquencies of old. He lit another cigarette and began to pace the room. He felt very tense. At last she glanced at him, then studied his face as if trying to read what he was thinking. When their eyes met he shook his head and said, "You silly girl!" She jumped up, almost knocked him off his feet, and started to shower him with tiny kisses on his hand and face. Then she dashed out of the room, and he heard clattering sounds. When she returned she was struggling under a tray piled high with bread, tinned food, and a bottle of apricot brandy. She set it all down on the table and started to eat ravenously. Bálint suddenly realized how hungry he was too. For some reason nothing at the hospital dinner had appealed to him, and now he set to it with a will. Blanka ate fast and greedily, swallowing large mouthfuls—food clearly hadn't passed her lips for some time, no doubt because of her fear. Then she set about the apricot brandy in the same way. He could see from the way she knocked it back that she was all too used to it. Soon she was so full she began to choke. He watched her and thought about the tribunal that lay in store for her. How could he possibly make anyone understand or accept what she had done? The girl had no awareness of the nature of her impulses; she never considered the consequences of her actions or the unbridled rage that all her life had overtaken her when she suspected that anyone looked down on her or rejected her. For them, she would be just another Stalinist informer. How could he possibly explain her reasons for bringing that ridiculous charge, or make the disciplinary panel understand, or believe in, what they had once shared in Katalin Street, and how deeply it would have affected her when he abandoned Irén? Smoking all the while, he racked his brains.

Finally he pulled the envelope from his pocket, the one he had been given at the hospital, and counted out the money. She watched him in silence, then touched the hundred-forint notes with awe. Bálint went over to the telephone and rang Szegi. They spoke in a kind of code, but Szegi gathered what he wanted quicker than Blanka had, and he roared with laughter when he heard that Bálint proposed sending his "sister" instead of himself and would be happy to pay in full if Szegi could guarantee that it would all work out. Szegi gave his word and said he would be outside the building at three in the morning. Bálint didn't wait to hear the obscene remarks about his sister-in-law and hung up.

Blanka struggled to grasp what he had in mind. He could see she was just as afraid of going as she was of staying. She hovered around him, miserable and indecisive, then suddenly sat down at his feet and placed her head in his lap. She whimpered for a while, then began to pack. Bálint had to throw out three-quarters of what she put in the bag. She wept and tried to grab it all back, disputing every item. Next, she wanted to say goodbye to her parents. Bálint said no. She had difficulty in seeing how important it was for them not to know that she had escaped to the West. Then she wanted to phone them to hear their voices for one last time, but that was refused as well, so she sat down and wept softly. She offered no thanks for the money Bálint had put in her bag. A solution that promised to place her beyond the reach of Timár's colleagues, and all her other responsibilities, weighed less with her than the terrifying uncertainty of where she might be going and what might happen to her once she got there. Bálint began to lose patience with her, and for a moment he was overcome with anger. She was being utterly irresponsible; she was ungrateful and stupid; he would do better to leave her to her fate and let Timár's bunch tear her to pieces, do whatever they wanted with her. He was now shouting at her, and she cowered in fear. He began to feel ashamed. Why was he shouting? This wasn't Irén, wise and clever Irén, it was only Blanka—a little mouse scuttling along the highway, terrified of the only path that led to safety because she had no idea what might be waiting there.

They ate once again, this time a more normal amount and less ravenously. Then she started to remake the bed. Bálint watched her struggling with the fresh linen and was again filled with pity for her. She was trying so hard, putting so much effort into it, but what in God's name was the point of putting clean sheets on a bed for this one last night?

There were sounds of shooting outside, still at a distance. The radio announcers seemed to have become deranged trying to keep up with everything that was going on. The two of them lay down side by side, as naturally as men and women do in times of disaster or in air-raid shelters during an attack. Blanka waited a while, then drew closer to him and stretched herself out as if inviting him to say what he wanted. He didn't want anything. "You don't have to pay me," he said almost angrily. "And you don't want it either." Her sigh of relief told him he had been right. For too long now fear had kept her from sleeping, and she was already dozing off. He lay beside her, fully awake and once again smoking. At one point he got up and made himself some coffee, finished the bottle of apricot brandy, and set the alarm for nine o'clock. He had to be at the hospital by ten. At two thirty he woke the girl. Just as in childhood, she was so drowsy she had difficulty standing up. He sprinkled her face with cold water, and she tottered off to the bathroom. He made her some tea, which she didn't drink, then she started to cry and tried yet again to smuggle some ridiculous knick-knacks into her bag. He smacked her hand sharply and took them out. She wanted to go in a blouse and skirt. He made her change into trousers, helped her dress, and draped her winter coat over her arm.

It was pitch-black when they left the apartment, and the world outside was completely still. The silence that reigned in the absence of traffic was more charged and more disturbing than if the tanks had been rumbling down the street. It took some time to rouse the concierge. Puffy-faced, her eyes half asleep, she opened the outer door. So far Blanka had not said a word, just gripped his hand tightly. Her teeth were chattering. "It's so cold," she said at last. She hadn't slept enough. Bálint knew that she was afraid and drew her closer to him, trying to warm her with his body. She started to mutter the kind of childish mantra they had once used to ward off danger, and again he felt like smacking her. The idiot, the stupid little goose—this time it was for Szegi not to come. She didn't want to go; she wanted to stay where she was and not have to confront the big wide world. So what would happen to her at the tribunal? When Szegi's truck finally stopped outside the building he had to push her away from him.

No one spoke. The truck was piled high with suitcases and people, children among them. Szegi whistled their old tune from the prison camp and Bálint made a surly reply, as if he felt too old for that sort of romantic nonsense. He threw

Blanka's suitcase on board, kissed the girl, and helped her up onto the truck. His last glimpse of her was by the reflected blaze of the headlights. Her hair was tucked under her bonnet and she was no longer crying. Szegi had made her sit beside him in the cab and had the good grace not to count out the notes that she pressed into his hand. In Bálint's eyes she was once again the little soldier, but stripped now of all anger and passion, she looked unutterably sad. Her rifle was nowhere to be seen.

THAT EVENING everything seemed particularly unreal. Pali came home early to tell us the latest news, but I couldn't concentrate on what he was saying. From the moment I heard that Bálint had been in the apartment I could think of nothing but him and myself, apart of course from Blanka and her fate. And I wasn't the only one who felt drawn back into that circle in which his life was inextricably bound up with mine, a life in which nothing had changed other than that, in the meanwhile, one of us had spent time as a prisoner of war, one had broken off with the other, one had been married and produced a child. My parents reacted to Pali's information with barely a word, and I knew that they too were thinking about Blanka and themselves, and about Katalin Street. No one said anything, but we all felt it. Pali blundered on regardless, until the poor fellow got on my nerves so much that I had to go into the dining room and start brushing out the fringes of the carpet just to get away from him.

I suspect now that he came to realize much earlier than the rest of us did—though it was only later again that we understood the full implications—that our attempt to live as a normal married couple in a conventional relationship was doomed to failure. We had never fully accepted him as one of the family, which was really sad: he was such an admirable and upright character. He was fond of my parents, as indeed they were of him, and he sincerely loved me, just as I loved him, up to a certain limit. But all through our marriage there had been things that we could never say to him, and aspects of his own life that simply didn't interest us.

That evening he must have spent quite some time feeling that, as so often before, we had again shut him out. There was nothing I could do to help, and I didn't dare attempt a private conversation with him about Blanka, who was then uppermost in everyone's mind, hiding in her apartment somewhere or other where they would soon catch her and punish her. We were preoccupied too with Bálint's unexpected appearance. His visit had made it impossible for us to deny that life without him had been insubstantial and unreal. My father was very pale, looking even more broken-down than usual. I knew for certain that he had not been in contact with Blanka since he had driven her out of the house, but also that he had never got over the memory of that day. For my part, I had long ceased to harbor the bitterness I first felt toward her. Indeed, what she had done turned out to have been useful, a source of relief. But for the fact that it had been Blanka, and specifically Blanka, who had brought his troubles upon him, Bálint might well have come back to me.

She and I began meeting shortly afterward. She would telephone me at the school and wait for me after work. Sometimes she even hung around outside the apartment hoping for a glimpse of our father. My mother spoke with her every second or third day. I met her initially in a café; then, when she was given an apartment, we saw each other there—though I had to warn her in the early days not to boast about the way she had jumped the queue. It was blood money, paid in return for Bálint's head. I often reduced her to tears this way, but she was always glad when I went to see her, and particularly touched when Pali came with me. She addressed my husband with as much decorum and respect as if she had been the Dame aux Camélias.

Naturally I had by then talked to Pali about Blanka, had told him what she had done, the simple details—everything that could be put into words. But looking back now, with the memories of our life together starting to fade, I can see that he never truly grasped the reality of what it all meant. For example, he never properly took in the fact that I had once had a serious love relationship that had come to nothing. He couldn't see how deeply it mattered to me; he thought it must have been just another childhood crush. Or again, he listened to the story of what happened to the Helds with real compassion but made no attempt to see a connection with the way the circumstances of their disappearance had affected, and might continue to affect, the lives of the rest of us. To him the three houses belonged to the past. He just couldn't understand what Katalin Street meant to the family.

On the night Bálint came back, my mother suddenly spoke out. I don't ever, in all our lives, remember having heard her use that particular tone. She could be quarrelsome or shrill, sly or charming, devious or flattering. This time she had something to say. She told my father that she was afraid for Blanka and that he should bring her back home. My father raised his head from his book, stared at her, and said nothing. From outside came the sound of distant gunfire.

Pali, who was much more able to judge the public mood from what he saw and heard at work than I was at the school, immediately supported her. Replying to him and ignoring my mother, my father said he had no need of advice, and he went on to expand his view of the matter: Blanka was an adult, she had made her bed and she should lie in it—nobody was going to kill her, unless she had committed any more crimes in the meantime—and if the verdict of history came down against her, she would just have to live with it. I expected my mother to burst into tears or throw a tantrum, but she did neither. She just went to the bedroom and shut the door behind her.

Pali called me away to bed, but I didn't follow him. I dithered about in the apartment, spinning out the time, waiting for him to fall asleep. I was completely off-balance. I needed time for reflection, and I racked my brains to think of a way of meeting Bálint again: I was convinced he must be living with Mrs. Temes. My father had also stayed up, not wishing to get into a discussion with my mother, and the two of us pottered about, postponing the moment. I'm sure he was just as aware of my reasons for being there as I was of his reluctance to go to bed. I rang the school caretaker, rousing him from sleep, and demanded to know if everything there was all right. It was. Unable to spin things out any longer I went to get ready in the bathroom. In the doorway I bumped into my mother. She had her coat on and a scarf over her head. She was about to leave the apartment.

Once again I was filled with astonishment at just how much the two of them loved Blanka, the one showing it by the harshness of his treatment of her and his total incapacity to forgive, the other so brave and so ready to take action on her behalf. At that time I still didn't realize that of all the people in the world I too loved Blanka the most, more than I loved anyone who ever had been or still was part of my life. More even than Bálint.

My father asked her, with some irritation, what she thought

she was doing. I took her coat from her and promised, as I gently pushed her back, that if she would stay at home I would go myself to fetch Blanka in the morning. I couldn't possibly allow her to leave the house that night, with shooting going on in the streets. My father heard my promise but pretended not to, and I saw a flash of joy cross his face. He was pleased that we had defied him, and I could see how intensely happy it made him to think that he might see his profligate daughter again. At this point my mother burst into tears. The noise woke little Kinga. Pali got out of bed, went and picked her up and brought her out to join the rest of us. Commotion reigned. He stood there, the child in his arms, staring at us like a young St. Joseph, without the faintest idea of what was going on.

Later I often thought back with a sense of guilt at the way I married him simply to put my own life in order, because I wanted a normal sexual relationship and someone to love me, to make up for having been rejected by Bálint. He certainly should not have waited until that evening when, during dinner, I told him, brightly and naturally and with no attempt to soften my words, that Bálint and I had decided to get married after all, and I would be leaving him. He should have been the one to leave me, but he just couldn't bring himself to do it. I often think of him now with a mixture of gratitude and yearning. He was a hundred times better as a husband than Bálint proved, and an altogether finer man. If there is indeed a life after death, I shall certainly be held to account for my marriage to him. It wasn't as if I had never given him anything, that is, up to the moment when I left him at a single word from Bálint. It was just that what I had been able to offer him amounted to very little. Almost nothing.

That night was an anxious one for all of us, but I was particularly on edge. Pali was every bit as conscientious as my father and nothing would have kept him from his place of work even in the most troubled of times, so he couldn't go with me to Blanka's. I knew that my father would never set foot over my sister's threshold—for him it was quite enough that he was allowing her to come back. Clearly I would have to go alone. Visiting her even in normal circumstances was always problematic. I knew what sort of life she led, and I listened to the allusions she made, the things she let slip, with all the awkwardness of a young woman in a respectable married relationship.

By this stage it had been a long time since my professional success had brought me any pleasure. A few years before, in the early fifties, both my father and I had been given awards. My father loathed everything to do with the personality cult but he nonetheless took a childish delight in these particular honors, imagining that in our case they were in recognition of the honest day's work we did, that they were an exception to the rule, a flicker of light in an hour of darkness. In fact it was my mother's response that made me realize that there was something odd about them, something not quite right. She let slip a few remarks, luckily in my presence and not my father's, about what a fine sister I had, and about the high-ranking official—she blushed the moment she said the word—who had taken her up and did whatever she wanted. I stared in horror at the box in which the medals lay glittering. I was a good teacher, truly conscientious, to say nothing of my father. We both deserved these honors, but I could no longer find any joy in them.

From then on I became deeply suspicious of all the little presents that found their way into our house from Blanka.

Most of them were unobtainable, and I wondered darkly about who might be her lover now: someone in the department of foreign trade, perhaps, or an important politician?

We set out early in the morning, I to the inner city, Pali to the waterworks. For the moment everything was quiet. Before leaving I had telephoned the central office and been told that lessons were still suspended, so I knew I had some time and would be able to arrive at school late. All the same I hurried, first to get the business with Blanka over quickly and then get to Mrs. Temes's. At the front door my mother had slipped a key into my hand. Again she had surprised me—I had no idea she had a key to Blanka's apartment. My father had behaved as if he knew nothing about where I was going and busied himself fumbling with the knobs on the radio, trying to catch the news. He paused for a second and looked at me as if he were attempting to imagine what his life would be like when finally he could see nothing at all. I left Pali at the corner of the street. The moment I found myself alone I began to feel less confident, but nothing untoward happened on the way. A truck coming from the market with a load of cabbages stopped beside me. The driver leaned out and asked if I was going to the city center, and if so, he would take me—I shouldn't be hanging around on the streets alone. I sat next to him, with the cabbages bouncing around behind us. The truck put me down just outside Blanka's window. The hated statue that had been erected just a few years earlier was no longer there. If I hadn't been so preoccupied with my own problems I would have paid more attention to that bizarre journey with the cabbages. I would have listened more carefully to what the driver was saying and realized that he was addressing me in the familiar form. Later on I called these images up in my memory—

the unexpected absence of the statue, what the driver was telling me, his use of the familiar "you"—and the strange, menacing silence everywhere.

Reaching the door of her apartment I suddenly felt afraid. The window in the door had been smashed and the gap stuffed with newspaper. I pressed the bell as we always did: three short rings. The door remained closed. Knowing Blanka I was hardly surprised. As a child, and even now as a grown-up, whenever she was frightened she always thought that she could hide safely inside a cupboard or under the bed. I was again astonished at my mother's foresight in giving me the key, and I turned the lock.

I stepped cautiously in, not expecting to find her straight-away. She would be in some hiding place, if she were alone, that is, and I tried to think of the sort of banalities that one might utter in the situation if she wasn't. I went on, through the hallway and the appallingly untidy sitting room, and opened the door to the bedroom. I stopped right there. The bed was unmade, and on it lay Bálint.

I forgot about Blanka, totally. It struck me later that if at that precise moment they had been dragging her away scream-ing in front of my eyes I probably wouldn't have noticed. I hadn't seen Bálint since the day I slammed my ring down in front of him and he walked out, and here he was now, lying naked in Blanka's bed, sleeping so deeply he hadn't even heard the doorbell. I sat down next to him on the edge of the bed and studied him. My father had conditioned me to think that it couldn't possibly be right for me, as a married woman, to be there, but a contrary reflex of my own made it seem absurd that such niceties should ever come between Bálint and myself—in fact I almost laughed. The notion that some-one like Pali should even exist seemed no less absurd.

I sat and waited for him to wake up. Knowing I was close to him made me so happy that I wanted to prolong the moment. Ridiculous thoughts filled my mind, about what he might say when he saw me—what if he had been married since Mrs. Temes last had news of him, and what if his wife came to visit us and sat down next to my husband and they told each other things that only they knew about the two of us, with Bálint and myself standing behind them laughing....

Bálint slept on, the peaceful slumber of the exhausted. I noticed that his features had become sharper, his face a little longer and older-looking. But seeing this made no difference to me. I wasn't interested in the signs of aging, only in Bálint himself.

I was still sitting there, oblivious to everything else, when the alarm suddenly went off. I jumped up, terrified, and he woke. The moment he opened his eyes he noticed me, stared in surprise for a moment, then looked at me steadily. He sat up, silenced the alarm, stretched, yawned, and said, "Hello, Irén," as if we had last met the day before. I made no reply.

I was hoping he would reach out and touch my hand, but he merely groped around the side of the bed, failed to find what he was looking for, and asked me to bring him a cigarette. His bag wasn't in the room, so I went into the next one. While I searched for it among the unbelievable chaos I heard him getting out of bed and moving around, obviously dressing. By the time I came back he was sitting in his shirt and trousers and pulling his socks on. He put on his shoes, came over to me, and gave me an affectionate kiss. I submitted, but didn't kiss him back. There was no point. It had been no more than a form of greeting, a kind of "good morning"—a chaste, brotherly kiss, appropriate for Henriette.

"I came to fetch Blanka," I said. "I'm taking her home."

He shook his head and waved his hand to show that she was gone. I stared in disbelief, afraid of what I feared. I simply couldn't imagine life without Blanka. Besides, if she had been taken away and had come to any harm, how could I look my father in the eye when I went home?

"She's defected," Bálint said. "I packed her off with a friend. She'll be over the border by now."

He had sent her. He of all people! Blanka, who had once sent him away? The relief that my sister was safe and beyond the clutches of the tribunal was equaled only by my confusion. Once again I was completely bewildered.

And now he came up to me, stood very close, and took my face in his hands. I closed my eyes, expecting a kiss. His mouth came very close to mine, then once again I no longer felt his breath, and he released me.

"It's so sad. You never could grasp the simplest facts," he said. "Life. Death. Clean water. Life isn't a schoolroom, Irén. There aren't any rules."

I glanced up at him. The look on his face had changed yet again. In his eyes I saw something not unlike pity, as if he knew that I was unwell and I didn't.

"You must reassure your parents. Tell them everything's fine. I'll look after her apartment. I'll move in here. I don't have anywhere to live, so I'll be fine right here—if I stay on in Budapest, and it looks as if I will. If I run out of money, I'll sell her things. Her knickers."

It was awful. I could never tell whether he was serious or joking. I automatically picked up the duvet, shook it out, and began to tidy the room. I couldn't stand the mess; every wardrobe door and every drawer was standing open.

"You're so perfect, you and your father," he said. "Wherever you go, order prevails. I often thought of you. After living in that house of yours everywhere else seemed filthy and disgusting. Shall I see you home?"

I didn't answer. I just stared at him, and my busy hands came to a stop.

"I have to be back at the hospital by ten. That's why I set the alarm. I'm going to be a bit late, but it doesn't matter. They don't mind what I do these days. I'll have to get you home while it's still possible, before it gets too late."

Again I looked at him, and our eyes met. He hauled his coat on and did up his tie.

"Aren't you going to wash?" I ventured timidly.

He roared with laughter and went on until he was almost choking. Again I stared in bafflement. I never for the life of me could think what to say when he was like this.

"When I get to the hospital," he said at last. "I do actually wash, but there's isn't time right now. I really must get you home safely. You never did know when to do things, Irén. Blanka was an idiot, a real idiot, but at least she knew that."

Before I knew it, I was out the door. He had taken my arm and was racing with me down the stairs. I had never asked, and Blanka had never told me, what happened between them in the shelter that night when Henriette died. Now I knew, and it no longer mattered. When he touched me I thought my breathing would stop. I hadn't realized just how much I still loved him, or how very little I loved my husband. As we walked I talked without ceasing. He had insulted me once before, and now after all these years he had done so again. Even his words of praise had been somehow patronizing. I could see all that but not feel it, and I told him everything about myself, everything I could put into words. He listened in silence, striding along. Out in the streets I could see more clearly how much he had aged over the past few years, how his hair was turning gray and he was starting to lose it, and his teeth were no longer as perfect as they had been. As we strode along Blanka was completely forgotten. All I could think of was why he hadn't asked me about the one thing that I hadn't mentioned, the subject to which I had never even alluded: did I really love Pali, and what sort of life did I have with him?

1961

ALTHOUGH she had come to dread meeting the people she had once known in Katalin Street, much preferring to be with them in the form she had re-created in her mind, she did nonetheless visit them often.

These encounters invariably distressed her, but she couldn't bear not seeing them, and if too long a time had passed since she had last done so she would become agitated and restless. She would then shut the door to the house she had constructed for herself in Katalin Street and leave the inhabitants to their various occupations—Mrs. Elekes with her pile of cushions, Mr. Elekes correcting homework, her mother busying herself about the place, her father in his consulting room, Mrs. Temes in the kitchen, the Major reading his newspaper in his study that smelled of leather, Irén at her schoolwork, Blanka chuckling away or crying, and Bálint in the garden. She bade them all farewell, promised she would not be away very long, closed the door on them, and they went on with their lives exactly where she had left them. Sometimes when she went back, she would shut herself away in her room, taking care not to show herself in case they should suspect something that only she knew about, something she too wanted to forget. At such times it was better just to closet herself away, because she often felt an overwhelming desire to talk to her father and mother and tell them how long they had before they would die, and the circumstances in which it would happen. She avoided the Major too: she was so afraid that she would let slip what she would in fact tell him later— when the two of them first met after their deaths—where he had fallen, and how upset he had been because he'd had absolutely no intention of dying, let alone of getting involved in a war, only he hadn't had time to explain that to the person who shot him. Mrs. Elekes she felt sorry for, seeing how she dreaded cleaning and tidying in Irén's room, and she helped her build up her collection of knickknacks. She urged Mr. Elekes to read as much as possible and kept bringing him more books, which she piled on his desk. She spent long hours chatting to Mrs. Temes, taking pleasure in the sharpness of her mind and the clarity of her thought.

Despite her awareness that meeting these people as they were now would always be painful, she was constantly drawn to their world. She was there when Bálint had his tribunal, there when Mr. Elekes ordered Blanka out of the house, and there when Irén got married, standing behind her in the church and noticing how grim she looked. She would have loved to have been her bridesmaid, but contrary to what they had all agreed on as children, Irén wore neither a corsage nor even a wedding dress. The wedding itself was as cheerless as one could possibly imagine. The bride's father had almost completely lost his sight, and instead of leading Irén to the altar had to be helped into the candlelit church. Blanka sat huddled in a corner, keeping herself away from the rest of the family, while a slim young man whom none of them knew made his blithe, naïve responses to the priest. Henriette was amazed that he couldn't see how out of place he was, standing there so proud and full of hope beside Irén. Henriette would have loved to see a wedding night, but she chose not to follow Irén home. The whole affair had been so depressing she knew she should just go back to Katalin Street and take to her bed. It had been nothing more than a bad dream. There, Irén and Blanka were still young girls who shared a bedroom, and if Irén was to be married to anyone it would be to Bálint. That thin, dark-haired young man in the church was simply an illusion. A figure in a dream.

Visiting Blanka's new home was always enchanting in itself. It was there that she had first seen the sea, and she would have taken an even greater pleasure in the dancing of the waves had she not found Blanka on the top of the cliff, choking in the heat, sobbing and crying out. The sight made her instantly want to rush back home. Blanka had become just another of the Henriettes that swarmed around the whitewashed house, and more of a prisoner than any of her family had ever been, despite possessing a real passport that could take her anywhere.

Hardest of all to bear were her visits to Bálint, though she yearned constantly to see him. In the prison camp, in the Elekeses' apartment, in the village, wherever he happened to be, he lived and moved like a high-wire artiste who had been crippled in a fall, been forced back into the ring, and was now going through his routines to the best of his ability but was so afraid of killing himself, and doing everything so joylessly, that far from entertaining the audience he was simply making them nervous. Though she had yearned unceasingly for him over the years, she never spent more than a few minutes with him. She had seen much more of him, and knew far more than Irén about his private life and his irregular relationships. Irén suspected only a fraction of what went on, and Henriette always felt ashamed when she saw him with other women. She could see what worthless creatures they were, and it upset her to think how many of them would sooner or later become his lovers.

What kept her retreating to the Katalin Street of her mind wasn't these women but the series of setbacks that dogged his steps at every point and threatened his career. No sooner would she be with him than she would flee from his side. She wanted to see him as a young man once again and be with him as he had been—so clever, so capable, and talented—and to hear Mrs. Temes, Mr. and Mrs. Elekes, and the Major talking about the wonderful career that awaited him. She was only truly contented and spontaneous when she felt close to him as the boy he had been, when she played the Cherry Tree game with him and the other two girls. Every time she found herself starting to be drawn again to the older Bálint she felt angry with herself, and she visited him only when the desire to see him in his bodily form overcame her better judgment.

Whenever she found herself beside one of these people in a shop, or bumped into one of them in the street, their reaction was always the same. They would glance at her briefly then look away, not particularly surprised or in any way troubled. None of them would believe for a moment that it was really her, Henriette, standing there or hurrying along beside them. The expression on their faces would soften for a moment, as if they had heard a fragment of song borne on the wind, an old song they had known and sung in child-hood and not heard since, and they were thinking how strange it was that a few bars of it should have come back to them just at that moment. When they failed yet again to recognize her or call her by her name, she hadn't the courage to address them, to explain that it really was her. She just stood there while the two of them looked at each other. It happened, quite often, that one of them would return her gaze, and sometimes they even stopped for a while. But they always moved on, visibly touched, with a distant look in their eyes, a look of wonder that the young girl they had just met should so strongly resemble someone they had once loved, someone they could never forget. But not once did they speak to her. Mrs. Elekes, Mrs. Temes, Mr. Elekes himself, and both Blanka and Irén had seen her in the street, countless times, but not for a second had they believed that it could be her, and these repeated encounters eventually discouraged her completely. It hurt her so much when they refused to acknowledge the reality of her presence and neither greeted nor spoke to her that for a time she gave up visiting them in a material form they might recognize.

The one person she had never shown herself to in bodily form was the one she actually went to see most often, Bálint. She thought that of all people it would be he, who had so loved her, who would know that it really was her. He hadn't panicked when he saw her lying there in the garden, and he wouldn't take fright now—he had simply taken a long, deep breath and sat down on the seat beside the fence. She was standing behind him, looking at her prostrate body and wondering how she might pull her skirt down. She had fallen between the rosebushes, and it had slid up, leaving her knees exposed.

She felt so confident that Bálint would find it natural that she should come back, and wouldn't react as the others had done, that year after year she had postponed the opportunity to reveal herself to him in bodily form. She wanted something from him. All her life she had wanted it, for so long without hope. She had seen him reject Irén, had seen Irén being married, and had thought that at last he might be hers. Then she would finally enjoy the peace of mind that would enable her to endure the life that would be hers forever. What she wanted was extremely naïve and no doubt immature rather than shameful, but it was still something she could never discuss with her mother, either as she was now or as the Mrs. Held she had re-created in Katalin Street. Finally she decided to tell Bálint himself, to let him know that at one time she had thought of him in a certain way, that she had longed for him ... and now she wanted to know whether, since Irén was no longer around, no longer part of his life, perhaps, had she still been alive, would it still be so unthinkable ... ? Timid and shy and fearful as she was, she spent ages preparing for this encounter. When she finally made her decision and set out from Katalin Street toward the hospital, she was sure the way her face kept changing from blood-red to deathly pale betrayed to everyone what was going on in her mind.

As always when she returned to the land of the living she was intimidated by the size of the city and the huge volume of traffic. She enjoyed walking, but there was a long way to go and she couldn't take any form of public transport because she had no money, only a handkerchief. Crossing over the bridge to Pest she realized there must have been an accident in the city center. A crowd was gathering, drivers were waving and gesticulating; a policeman had asked one of them for his papers and he had produced a whole sheaf of them, which the officer was now carefully going through. She found it amusing, but it brought home to her that she had none of her own, and she quickened her pace. All her official documents had been left at the old house and then destroyed. As for those of Mária Kis, even if Mrs. Held hadn't burned them they would have been of no use to her since everyone now carried the new red certificates of identity.

When she finally reached the hospital she was told to wait for Bálint, who would appear shortly. Outside the entrance there was an old statue of St. John surrounded by benches, and from there she kept an eye on the entrance, glancing every so often at the clock on the façade. When she at last caught sight of him she felt a twinge of fear. He wasn't alone. She recognized his companion. It was Timár. Luckily Timár got into a car, and Bálint set off on his own. She followed him. She was almost as nervous as she had been at the Major's thirty-fifth birthday celebration, when, holding the shield, she had fainted from a mixture of happiness and sheer terror. Now it was precisely the thing on which she had pinned her hopes, the thing she had come back to achieve, that made it a thousand times more difficult for her to approach him.

He was walking very quickly. He had done so all his life, and she had always had difficulty keeping up with him. Now it was as if he were running away from her, which of course was absurd, as he hadn't even seen her. She struggled to catch him up and by the time she drew level on the pavement she was panting heavily. Her heart was beating so strongly she feared she might be ill. She tried to calm herself down, telling herself not to worry since she *couldn't* be ill, it wasn't *possible*. But her chest was heaving. For the last several meters she had been positively running, and it was the sound of her little gasping noises that finally made him notice her. He turned his head to look, glanced at her briefly, then turned away and carried on walking. "He doesn't believe what he saw," she thought. But she wasn't upset. She hadn't thought it would be any different. She knew she would have to give him time to realize what was happening.

But he walked on. Occasionally he looked round, as if to confirm that whoever had been there was still there, and promptly quickened his pace, showing not the slightest intention of either stopping or speaking to her. By now she was almost running. When he suddenly turned down a side street she knew she had hoped in vain. He hadn't believed, any more than the others had, that it was her beside him and not some stranger wanting to accost him. It made her so miserable she sobbed in despair.

He went into an espresso bar. In the doorway he bumped into a woman, clearly a stranger. She smiled at him. He smiled back joylessly, and she asked his pardon.

Henriette pulled herself together and peered through the window. She knew that if she let the moment slip she would never again have the courage or strength to approach him or even show herself to him in a form he could comprehend. "Patience," she told herself. "This won't be easy. And it won't be easy for him. I can't run away now. It would all be over."

She gazed at the young man, and around the café. She had never been in one of these places before. In the old days there were only coffeehouses and patisseries; less coffee was drunk and by fewer people—it wasn't then the fashion. She stared in wonder at the strangely shaped cups, the espresso machine, and at Bálint, who was now sitting at a table on his own. He was looking at her through the window, returning her gaze. She hesitated a moment longer, made her decision, and went in to meet him. She was terrified. She walked slowly up to him and sat down at the table. Once again they were face-to-face.

Still he said nothing. Eventually he reached out and moved his doctor's briefcase to a chair farther away. She realized he was making a place for her to sit next to him. She breathed a sigh of relief, moved over, and waited for him to speak her name.

The arrival of the waitress cast a shadow across the table. She was asking what they wanted. Henriette glanced down at her lap, and his eyes followed hers. She had no purse, no handbag, no gloves. Now he spoke for the first time, to order two coffees. When they arrived she sniffed hers gently: it had a powerful, heavy aroma. She didn't touch it. She didn't want to drink, she didn't want anything to eat or drink, and she simply stirred it.

At last he spoke. He wanted to know what she wanted. She said nothing. She just looked at him.

"Drink up your coffee and clear out of here," she heard him say. "There might be a police raid, and they'd arrest you."

Another raid? What sort of raid? A moment of fear, then she smiled. No one would ever harm her again. Bálint finished his cup without another glance at her and paid the bill. Seeing him about to leave she stood up. The surprised waitress asked her why she hadn't drunk her coffee. She made no reply and followed Bálint out, keeping close behind him.

As children they had often played a game where they were supposed to be someone else. She usually came last. When it was her turn she could never think of anything to prove that she was that person, as the rules required. Once again she had the feeling, the shameful feeling of old, that she couldn't make anyone believe who she was, but this time the shame was familiar and nostalgic, tinged with sweetness. She was again walking beside him, still very nervous, and still hoping that he would eventually stop and say her name. He had, after all, made her sit down at his table and ordered her coffee.

He complained constantly as he walked, the way he always had whenever something was bothering him. He kept telling her to go away, to leave him in peace: in God's name, couldn't she leave an exhausted man alone? She understood the words, but the meaning went over her head and failed to penetrate her consciousness. She followed him devotedly, and when she realized that he was going to the apartment he had taken over from Blanka, she smiled to herself. Of course, that was why he had been so silent in the café, and why he had said so little out in the street in front of strangers, and why he was saying such odd things now. They needed to be away from other people before they could really be together.

When they arrived at the entrance to the building he stopped, and she knew she had been right. He studied her for a while, then said, "All right, come on up." As she ran up the stairs beside him she wondered what she would say to him when the time finally came. Until he actually told her that he knew who she was there was nothing she could say. When they got to the door he spoke again, just as he was about to open it, but it made no more sense than what he had said earlier. It seemed to have no connection with the two of them or their real relationship. Why, at that precise moment, did he tell her, "I don't have very much money"?

But he was the first, the only one, who had allowed her to go home with him, had actually invited her in! It felt very familiar walking through the apartment. She had been there often enough, even if it was in a form he wouldn't have been able to see. She went straight to the table where the Major's photograph stood, then glanced up at the wall behind the sofa, at the portrait of the Major's wife that Mrs. Temes had rescued from the old house. Bálint watched her closely, seeming not very pleased by the fact that she had approached and greeted his father and mother, that she should take so much interest in his parents.

But he said nothing. He still hadn't told her his name or

asked her to sit down. Perhaps he didn't know how to begin? Seeing her again couldn't be easy for him—on the last occasion she had been lying dead in the garden—but she was puzzled by the way he kept spinning out the time with these trivial actions. How could she help him, make it easier for him to find the opening words? He was behaving very oddly. It wasn't at all how she had imagined their first meeting would be.

He emptied his wallet and started counting out his money. He really didn't have much on him. He put a fifty-forint note to one side and looked at her. She returned his gaze and smiled, waiting for him to say something, something personal. The smile died on her lips as she saw him undo his tie, take off his coat, and disappear into the bathroom to get undressed. He came back in his dressing gown, with slippers on his bare feet. Under the dressing gown he was naked.

She just stood there, in the middle of the room, her hands clenched, saying nothing. She was deathly pale, hardly able to breathe.

"What are you waiting for?" he demanded. "You can take your own clothes off. I don't like messing around with that sort of thing."

It was altogether more than she had bargained for. If he had addressed her as herself, as the Henriette he had at last recognized, then perhaps she might have gone with him. But he hadn't. Now she knew that he wasn't speaking to her as herself, and she understood what he had taken her for. If he hadn't done so by now, he clearly never would realize who she was.

She stood there, motionless. He reached for a cigarette, but there was no time for him to light it. She went up to him, much closer than she had so far, and touched him gently with the tips of her fingers. He took her hand, even as he understood that what he had been expecting wasn't going to happen. There would be no lovemaking. For some reason this queer little girl had changed her mind. He wasn't particularly bothered by that. He hadn't really wanted her. He just hadn't had the heart to turn her away, she was so like Henriette. And how could he tell her that he would have slept with her only out of kindness, because she was so like someone he had once loved, loved probably more than anyone in his life? She would never have understood. She was interested only in the money—what else was she after? She had nothing, not even a handbag. What he couldn't work out was why, after coming all that way with him, she had then changed her mind.

He didn't want to take her to bed, but he longed to kiss her. She declined. She turned away, walked around the room once more, then again came up to him, so close that he could feel her breath. Once again she placed her fingers on his face momentarily, then, still as silent as she had been out in the street, she started toward the door. He thought she might have changed her mind again, that she was going to the bathroom to get undressed, and he suddenly realized he wanted her. He really wanted her—but with an accompanying sense of shame, as if he had just been given a sister and physically desired her. The idea was at once horrifying and strangely alluring.

He heard her footsteps go quickly past the bathroom, then the click of the lock in Blanka's front door. There was no way he could run after her. She was already out in the stairwell and he was still in his dressing gown and barefoot. He opened the window and leaned out, so that he could at least watch her leave. She was just going out into the street.

She was sobbing, sobbing as she ran. She ran awkwardly, without any rhythm, the way Henriette used to. "Perhaps she's hungry," he thought. "She had no money." He realized he should have given her something; she shouldn't have been allowed to leave empty-handed, he could at least have given her the fifty-forint note. He went back to the window and crumpled the note into a ball to throw after her. But he was too late. By the time he had leaned out and looked around for her, the square was empty.

I LEARNED later that he had gone first to the school and been told where he could find me: I was on my way to the exhibition with my class and might already have arrived. As far back as he could remember, he said, he had never been inside one of these places, and as he set off to find us he was glad to have the chance to see the famous collection at the same time. I was already in the building when I spotted him, standing in one of the rooms among the statues, and I was very happy to see him there. My body registered that pleasing sense of intimacy that had long shed any charge of sexuality. In that respect we had both put our lives in order; this was more like the instinct by which animals born blind recognize one another, the shared memory of a collective dream. I was always happy when I saw Bálint.

We didn't speak to each other immediately. I had my hands full. I couldn't leave the class to their own devices, and I needed to get a sense of the contents of the different rooms. So I went from one to the other, looking about, with an increasing sense of dismay. My aesthetic preference is for the smoothness of bronze and polished marble, and those calm, serene, noble faces, and I was confident that the pupils would understand and respond to those perhaps even better than I would. Instead, I had stood, in something verging on horror, before the piece that was the pride of the exhibition, staring at its shapeless contours, the twisted heads and the sightless gaze in their eyes that were not eyes but holes carved in stone in place of eyes, vacant spaces that held the real meaning of those faces. None of them had eyes, ears, or noses.

He was obviously waiting for us to be able to move away somewhere and talk. Ever since Blanka's departure we had met regularly if infrequently, but we had never been together for more than a few minutes without a member of the family being with us. Bálint liked Pali and enjoyed talking to him: Pali's being there troubled him so little that at first it rather offended me. He found my little daughter Kinga amusing and handled her rather better than her father did, who was always the overanxious parent whose ceaseless attention she found rather annoying. A few days earlier Bálint had spent the whole afternoon with us, so bumping into him in the gallery wasn't a complete novelty, though an even more delightful surprise for that. I signaled with my eyes to my colleague to ask if she could manage without me and she nodded her affirmation; the children were quiet and taking an interest in the statues. So I went over to him and as usual started to talk about Blanka: we'd had a letter from her the day before. He stopped me in my tracks. We could talk about that later. He wasn't there by chance. He had come because he wanted to discuss something with me, then and there if possible.

We sat down on one of the benches, he at a short distance from me, so that I could see both him and the statues. There was now a different expression on his face, a curious look of reconciliation, of things having been resolved. It annoyed me just a little. Bálint's face always betrayed his changing moods, whether of anger or mockery, intimacy or coldness, and I had seen him in this state of mind before. There was the same unfeeling detachment he had shown when he told me he had been put to work in an office yet again, not as a result of any particular complaint made against him or because of his class origins but because it had apparently been decided that, in the end, he just wasn't a good enough doctor to be in charge of a ward: he supposedly lacked something, some God-given gift, that would have made him a good physician. He clearly didn't see it as anything tragic. He talked about the whole business as if it had happened to someone else. My parents' response showed that they were much more upset about it than he was. But I knew what lay behind his display of resignation.

I didn't have to wait long for the message he had come to deliver. It was couched in the simple terms one might use for ordering a book. He had decided to marry me: I was to divorce Pali and live with him.

I didn't move. I simply turned my gaze away from him and back to the statues. Near us, on a low plinth, stood three marble columns with a large stone ball entitled *The Warrior*. It was just a torso, one of those strange, formless ones that have a head but no face and no limbs. It was grotesque, but, God knows why, it projected an extraordinary force. I looked at it and made no reply. I didn't think he expected one. He knew, as we all did, perhaps even my husband himself, that Pali's coming to live with us had been a sort of accident. He lived among us and in our apartment but no one had ever taken him seriously, not even my father, with all his views on the sacredness of marriage. Bálint also knew that Kinga wasn't a true token of love between us, the romantic fulfillment of our life together: we had simply wanted someone through whom we could satisfy our need for caressing and petting without feeling embarrassed. We might as well have bought a puppy.

He didn't reach over to take my hand and I didn't offer it. Some years before I had asked him what he felt when he suddenly saw Timár's car pulling up outside the house in the village and he was told he was free to return to Pest, and that everyone knew he had been innocent all along. He shrugged his shoulders, as if reluctant to reply, then gave me that look I knew so well of old, the one that told me that this was clearly one of those things I would never understand, and he muttered something about it having meant nothing to him. "So being rehabilitated counts for nothing?" I had asked indignantly, and my father, who was with us at that moment, remarked that one should never be ungrateful or cynical. "I'm not cynical," he retorted with irritation; and he went on, in a rather louder voice than usual, "It meant nothing to me at the time. It's something neither of you would ever understand."

Well, I understood now.

I lowered my eyes. I didn't want the children to see tears streaming from them. I felt his fingers closing around my wrist. At that moment, perhaps for the first time in our lives, he had no idea what was going on in my mind. His touch was warm, and its gentle pressure told me exactly what he was thinking: "Look, I know how happy you are. Everything that has kept us apart has now changed, is behind us. Show your happiness not through tears but with your whole heart, the way you once knew how to." For the first time in our lives he just couldn't see that I had given way not to joy but to despair—despair for myself and for him. If I was weeping so profusely I could no longer bear to control myself as the place and the circumstances required, it was because it was such a long time since I had last loved him.

The thought was no less horrifying than the statues standing around us. If I could I would have plucked it out like a splinter from under a fingernail. I saw in an instant that Pali was the only solid element in the concentrated unreality in which we were all struggling and drowning. My father had been reduced to helplessness and my mother slaved away day and night and lived in a permanent state of nerves: she and I were the only ones who were still what we had always been. The old houses in Katalin Street had vanished. Everyone who had known us as we were had taken refuge in illness, like Mrs. Temes, or disappeared to some distant island, like Blanka, or been killed, like the Major and the Helds. But Pali was real and true, even if none of us acknowledged that or took him seriously; perhaps even he didn't think of himself as a real member of the family. Now he would no longer be there, and his leaving the apartment would shut off the one route through which we might ever follow him. It would mean that now we would never be able to escape. Bálint had come back and blocked the way. He had struggled on for so long on his own and finally come to see that without us he would never find what he had always wanted, something from the time when the two of us were children. Only through us could he make his way back to Katalin Street. We were the only ones who remembered that time when everything in his life held hope and promise.

I lost all interest in who was watching or what people might think of me. For the first time since I had become a teacher I stopped caring about what the pupils might say—that they had seen me sitting on a bench unable to hold back my tears. Bálint moved closer to me. By now he wasn't simply holding my hand; he also had his arm around my shoulder. I was thinking about how all my life I had been preparing for just this moment, the moment when I would become his wife, and now here we were, so close to achieving that, closer than we had been even on the day Henriette died. The war had ended, there was no more bombing, and it was now more than ever possible to make plans that might actually come to something. But we had both grown older, he no longer loved me with the same soulful intensity that he once had, my own feelings for him had cooled and were exhausted. We would be setting out on life as traveling companions aboard a ship that might be blown God knows where, clinging to each other and exchanging our sad memories, having known the same sunny uplands and what it had been like living there before we had been plucked away to sea; both having seen the same blue sky shining, before the thunder broke.

I just sat there. In my mind I was bidding farewell to calm and tranquility. I was saying goodbye to Pali whom I loved and beside whom life was simple and comfortable. He had never asked more of me than I was able to give, had never once pried into my silences and secrets. By now I was no longer crying. My tears had run dry. I was numb with fear. Bálint looked at me, and there was a tenderness in his eyes, and pity. He was used to my not understanding him and had often made fun of me. Even in the days when we were so madly in love he had complained about how little I was able to read his mind. Now, as I gazed back at him, I would have loved to tell him that perhaps for the first time in our lives I knew exactly what was going on inside his head and why he felt so sorry for me. I also knew what he had left unsaid, something he should have added to his request: "It is a corpse I am offering you, Irén, not the person you once loved. The man you will marry is an empty shell, just so much empty air."

I listened, utterly chilled by this moment that had overtaken and overwhelmed us both. I should have told him not
to concern himself about me, to pity himself rather than
pity me. Irén Elekes was no more. She might never have
existed. While I had Blanka at my side I had felt complete,
whole, perfect. I believed, as she did, that I had been born
to be that way. Then one day I realized that I had never been
either what people thought me or what I had imagined
myself to be: I had believed in it only because there was
someone who loved me so much that she took all my sins
upon herself, even before I—had I not been a slave to con-
vention and essentially a coward—might have been able to
understand what they would be. But Blanka was gone, leaving me to perpetrate my crimes by myself, and the people I
lived with kept out of my way in fear and trembling. Only
Pali was able to put up with me, because he had no memory
of my younger self. I sat and contemplated myself and the
rest of us, in the new apartment, where Bálint would be
coming to live in the hope of recovering the peace and calm
he had known in his father's house, and I saw him standing
there in amazement at me shouting at my mother, hurling
a plate to the floor, slapping little Kinga when she got on my
nerves, or back in the kitchen utterly exhausted after a long
day at school, brandishing a cup at the men that someone
had forgotten to wash and complaining to one and all about
the miserable life I led.

So there we sat in silence. Neither of us spoke the words
we should have, and this time it was I and not Bálint who
saw that whatever we did say would change nothing. I looked
at the statues standing around us, those strange forms that
were little more than blocks of stones piled on top of one
another rather than carved, and I imagined them directing

their eerie, unseeing gaze at us. Then I turned my head away. I had heard Bálint heave a sigh, or rather not a sigh but a yawn, a yawn not of boredom but of sheer exhaustion, and I suddenly realized that I wanted to yawn too. I was inexpressibly weary. It was like finding myself able to sit and rest at last after years, decades of being pursued and hunted down.

We said nothing about the practical arrangements, and nothing about the details. We knew it wasn't urgent, that there would be plenty of time. Pali would see to whatever had to be done and make it all happen with the minimum of bloodshed. My pupils were lining up. When I went back to join them, Bálint went with me, as if he couldn't bear to leave me alone for a minute. I conducted myself admirably. I spoke thoughtfully and clearly, and even added a few remarks about the displays. Conscious that I might have been seen crying on the bench, I did my best to make them forget my loss of composure even as I deplored the sort of strength that could summon up the self-control needed to force oneself to be what other people expected when I would have much rather have stayed as I am: I was tired of everything and everyone, above all of Bálint. We set off, and I knew that never again, as long as we lived, would I really be myself, and that what had happened, and was going to happen, would be meaningless, pointless, and far too late.

My colleague walked at the head of the group, the two of us at the back. It was midday, the sun was shining brightly, and as we left the gallery we chatted about the weather. Our distorted shadows writhed on the pavement, and I watched them flitting along beside us in the strong sunlight. Two vast blocks of stone stalked ahead. Their shadows had neither eyes, nor hands, nor feet. They were just limbless trunks.

1968

THE TREES were very old, but every spring their branches were thick with leaves and they showed no sign of disease. The leaves never fell early because the people in the street loved the trees, and every evening, in the dog days of summer, they threw buckets of water over the roots. Henriette walked down the street more often than the others did, and she was the first to notice that the avenue was being cut down. When she got home that evening she told her parents and the Major about it. The news greatly upset her parents, as the trees had a special place in their memories, so she decided that the next time she went home she would resurrect them: the street looked maimed without them. "It won't be possible while they're still taking them down," the Major advised. "You must wait until they're all gone. Only then will you be able to restore them." So she waited until the tree surgeons and their machines had finished, until nothing was left of the row of trees and the work on all three houses had been completed. Then she put everything back, houses and trees together. The Major had been right. The trees came back at once, took up their old places, and submitted to the laws of the seasons, just as they always had.

A few weeks later more building began, and again she started to worry. Henriette knew nothing about overpopulation and shortages of building land, but now she was afraid that after the trees the part of the riverbank that hadn't been built on would be next and the view from their houses of the Danube glittering between the trunks would be lost. The street would be completely changed. So far they had built only on the left side, never on the right. She felt it would be very hard to have to wait until all the construction work had been completed and normal life had resumed in her three houses before she could make it all disappear again and restore the old view of the riverbank.

By the time the houses on the other side of the road were finished their beloved view of the Danube had indeed gone. It was as if an enormous hand had gathered it up and whisked it away. The city planners declared Katalin Street an area of special historic interest, and a row of single-story houses appeared, facing Castle Hill and built in a style that harmonized with the existing buildings. They even had gardens. They weren't as large as those of the houses on the left-hand side, but they went all the way down to the river. You could see newly planted trees and flowers through the low wire fencing.

Henriette loved the Danube. Whenever she was back in her bodily form and found herself walking along the bank, she felt compelled to observe the shape the street was taking. She would stop from time to time, peer over fences, and watch the new residents sunbathing, playing cards in the garden, all the usual everyday events—the postman ringing a doorbell and handing over an envelope that would be instantly torn open; someone carefully prizing the cap from a bottle of beer and taking a hearty swig, leaving a line of foam across his lips.

Occasionally these people would speak to her as she stood looking in. This delighted her but it also left her feeling embarrassed. The young men sometimes teased her, but she never reacted and after a while they always left her alone. On one occasion some teenagers hit her with a football. The boy responsible never apologized, he just asked her to throw it back. She did and said nothing, but as it sailed through the air she suddenly remembered how much she had loved playing with a ball, and the next time she came she brought her own with her from the house in Katalin Street and bounced it ahead of her, with gentle taps of the hand, all the way along the waterfront. The place smelled of water, river water. She wandered up and down beside the Danube, bouncing her red ball as she went.

Gradually she came to know the residents of the new houses on the other side of the street.

In the officer's house there was a boy, a tough-looking fellow with blond hair, who was often in the garden when he wasn't doing his homework. Next door there were two girls, a quiet one with dark hair and a smaller one who never stopped talking. They often played with the boy, losing themselves so completely in the game that Henriette really envied them, and sometimes she made her ball bounce into their garden so that the game would stop while they returned it. Occasionally she caught sight of the parents, the officer leaning on the fence explaining something and laughing, and the father of the girls, an incompetent-looking short-sighted little man who was always fussing about while his wife sprawled on a deck chair reading glossy magazines, or getting something for the children to eat.

One day Henriette had a strange experience with this woman. She was standing in the street looking in and watching the girls eating, when the idle, slovenly mother unexpectedly came up to her and handed her a doughnut over the fence. The plate was chipped, and it wasn't exactly clean. The woman smiled at her and told her that as she had shown so much interest in it she might at least try one. Henriette took it, since it had been offered, and stared at the doughnut in confusion, no more able to thank the woman than to explain why she didn't want it, or why she had been standing there watching. As soon as the woman turned her back she broke the doughnut into small pieces and scattered it on the water. The fish darted towards it, large brown fish, their mouths gaping wide to snatch it. The children saw what she had done and the younger girl began to shout angrily about what sort of idiot would throw her doughnut in the river. The older one nodded her head reproachfully, and the boy ran out, grabbed the plate from her hand, and told her she needn't expect anything from them again in a hurry, so she could clear off and go to the devil. It was a long time before she dared bounce her ball outside their house again.

There was another house on the new side of the road where no one had spoken to her yet. It stood empty, and whenever she didn't want either to stay in Katalin Street or to be where the Soldier was, she went there instead and dawdled about, bouncing her ball.

One day she arrived home earlier than usual. Mrs. Held had upset her. The day before she had gone off to a spa with her nurse, a place she used to visit in childhood, and had come back in one of those ridiculous old-fashioned bathing suits people used to wear for paddling in the sea. Henriette hated it when she regressed like that, and she also had a horror of the nurse and the way she talked down to her mother. She was so desperate to see the real Mrs. Held that she almost hurled herself into the kitchen. She had heard her mother humming inside, and she went and nuzzled up to her for ages until she had calmed down and washed her mind clean of the image of that unreal child with the bucket full of shells.

Mrs. Held had put some apricots into a bowl, but Henriette left them there and went on to finish her usual tour of inspection. Later on, when she was absorbed in the old children's game in the garden and had completely forgotten about them, her mother signaled to her from the kitchen window that they still hadn't eaten the fruit. Bálint went inside to fetch the bowl and ran back with it to the others. Blanka snatched it from his hand and started to divide the contents up, and Irén put some vine leaves on the steps to serve as plates. Blanka counted out the apricots in a singsong rhythm: one-two-three-four. Henriette looked on with the delight that filled her every time she noticed that this Blanka had included her in the share—all too often in their childhood she had forgotten that the fruit belonged to everyone and divided it into three, as if Henriette simply didn't exist. The dentist's drill hummed away, Blanka handed out the fruit, counting as she did: one-two-three-four. The sun was shining brightly.

They sat down on the bottom steps and Blanka immediately started to wolf hers down. That was when Henriette first heard the noise. She didn't take much notice at first, but after a while it struck her as odd to hear something other than the whining of the drill. This was quite different—a scraping and bumping sound, as if large objects were being lifted and dumped on the ground. It seemed inconceivable that her mother would be moving anything around in the house that would make so much noise, so she ran inside to take a look.

Mrs. Held was in the sitting room. She heard Henriette come in and turned her head.

"What's that sound?" Henriette asked.

Mrs. Held replied that it was probably just the ship. There was one sailing along in front of them. "Look how beautiful the Danube is today, and what an unusual blue. That's a very large ship. What kind is it?"

Henriette stood beside her, following her gaze. From the window she could see the line of trees and the new houses in between them. They were in the way, and the river was no longer to be seen. The door of the last vacant house across the road was open, and workmen were moving in and out of the porch, carrying furniture from a truck. The furniture would pause briefly at the door, then continue on its way and disappear into the house.

"Can you see the flag? It's a German ship," said Mrs. Held. "I wonder what they have on board."

She saw furniture and suitcases, and the residents of the new street. The shortsighted man, the officer, and an unknown woman were standing at the door, with the slovenly woman beside them, holding a bag. The children were capering about between the boxes and odds and ends, enjoying the general chaos, then suddenly they started to run. A car was turning into the street, near the church. They ran in front of it, then followed it all the way back to the front door. To their delight a man got out, with a little girl on his arm. He set her down, and the two girls, the one with large eyes and the little blonde, immediately took charge of her and raced with her into the garden. The boy went after them, at a slower pace, and the grown-ups watched them, laughing.

"There's another ship," said Mrs. Held. "Go and call Bálint, so he can see it too."

Henriette went out, not into the garden but straight across the road to the newly built side, and followed it along to the end. She turned the corner next to the church, went down to the waterfront, and stood beside the fence where she usually played with her ball. The garden was full of lumber—armchairs taken outside and piled high with clothes, stacks of books, bed linen, and a bench heaped with cushions, pillows, bed linen, and towels.

The boy saw that she was back again and ran to the fence. The others followed and they all stood facing one another. The workmen were now carrying a white enameled glass sideboard toward the foot of the staircase, and a dentist's chair, with the drill dangling down like a snake. The smaller girl put out her tongue at Henriette.

"It's that girl with the ball," the boy said. "The dumb idiot who likes feeding fish."

"Shush," said the dark-haired girl. "We don't even know her."

"Dumb idiot," the little blonde repeated. "Dumb idiot, who likes playing with her ball!"

"Get the hell out of here," the boy said.

"Shush," said the dark-haired girl again. "You shouldn't say things like that."

Henriette barely heard her. Her eyes were on the little one and the furniture. Beyond the girl, in the middle of the garden and in front of the piles of bed linen, she could see the footstool. She couldn't make out the pattern on the upholstery because the underside of the frame was toward her. She stood with her face distorted by the pain of concentration. Voices came from inside the house, calling the children back. The feet of the newly arrived child seemed to tremble, as if she wanted to go back and be with them. She was a timid little thing, with pale skin and dark eyes.

"Let's go," said the boy. "We're in charge of this kid. We'd better take her back. Come on."

The blond girl dashed off, her shoes slapping on the flag-stones as she ran between the piles of bed linen and disappeared through the door. The dark-haired girl followed her slowly, as if in two minds. There was a pleasing calmness about the way she walked, a kind of gentle dignity, though she could hardly have been ten years old. The new arrival looked up at Henriette, hesitantly. The boy was still there.

"Are you still looking at the idiot?" he asked.

The little girl said nothing.

"She'll throw you in the river too, like her doughnut."

Henriette didn't understand what he meant by that, but the remark disturbed her, it was so strange and terrifying. She gazed at each of them in turn.

The boy started to lose patience.

"All right, stay there then. If you get bored, we're inside the house."

He thudded off.

The child looked round and realized that she was alone at the fence with a total stranger. She panicked, and the blood rushed to her face. Fearing that she might run off at any moment, Henriette put her hand through the wire fence and touched her. The little girl allowed the touch, but acted as if it was hurting her, and Henriette pulled her fingers away. She had no idea whether her touch was like other people's or whether it might possibly be bad for the child to be touched by her. From inside the house she could hear laughter, an argument going on, and a regular stamping sound coming from somewhere, as if there was a game in progress, with singing and dancing.

"What's your name?" she asked the child. It was the first time she had spoken since she had been killed, and she wasn't sure she would be understood. The little girl didn't reply.

She just looked at her in wonder, as if uncertain whether she was allowed to talk to a stranger; her mouth opened and the lips glistened, but before she could say anything the other children had darted back along the garden path, seized her hand, and run off with her and through the now empty doorway.

The furniture, the suitcases, and the bed linen vanished. Someone closed the door from the other side, and she could no longer see either the workmen or the grown-ups. Now, as from a great distance, she saw the children holding hands in a ring. The little one must have been too inept, because she hadn't been invited in. She stood apart, watching the other three. Henriette leaned on the fence and listened. She wanted to hear what they were singing. But they noticed that she was still there. The dance was abandoned. The boy bent down to pick up a stone and made as if to throw it. She ran and found herself on the waterfront again, then beside the church, then disappearing through the Helds' front door.

That day she arrived back at her usual place of residence rather earlier than usual. There was nobody around: not the Major, not her grandparents, not the Helds. There was only the Soldier. They stared at each other for a while, then he asked her once again how he could find his way home. For the first time since they had met she looked at his face with neither fear nor horror. It was a simple face, young, a little stupid. Once again she said nothing.

IN EVERYONE'S life there is only one person whose name can be cried out in the moment of death.

Bring Blanka home!

PRONUNCIATION GUIDE

KATALIN — The *a* as in *salt*, with a slight stress on first syllable (Hungarian for *Catherine*)

ELEKES — *Elekesh* with a slight stress on first syllable

TEMES — *Temesh* with a slight stress on first syllable

BIRÓ — *Bee-raw* with a slight stress on first syllable

IRÉN — *Ee-rayn* with a slight stress on first syllable

BÁLINT — *Baa-lint* with a slight stress on first syllable (Hungarian for *Valentine*)

BLANKA — The *a*'s sounded as in *salt*, *Baltic*, with a slight stress on first syllable

LAJOS — *Loy-osh*, with a slight stress on first syllable

PALI — The *a* sounded as in *salt*, *Baltic*, and with a slight stress on first syllable

TIMÁR — *Tee-mar* with a slight stress on first syllable (not the second)

KIS — *Kish*

OTHER NEW YORK REVIEW CLASSICS

For a complete list of titles, visit www.nyrb.com or write to:
Catalog Requests, NYRB, 435 Hudson Street, New York, NY 10014

J.R. ACKERLEY My Dog Tulip*
J.R. ACKERLEY My Father and Myself*
J.R. ACKERLEY We Think the World of You*
RENATA ADLER Pitch Dark*
RENATA ADLER Speedboat*
AESCHYLUS Prometheus Bound; translated by Joel Agee*
LEOPOLDO ALAS His Only Son *with* Doña Berta*
CÉLESTE ALBARET Monsieur Proust
DANTE ALIGHIERI The Inferno
KINGSLEY AMIS Dear Illusion: Collected Stories*
KINGSLEY AMIS The Green Man*
KINGSLEY AMIS The Old Devils*
KINGSLEY AMIS Take a Girl Like You*
ROBERTO ARLT The Seven Madmen*
U.R. ANANTHAMURTHY Samskara: A Rite for a Dead Man*
WILLIAM ATTAWAY Blood on the Forge
W.H. AUDEN (EDITOR) The Living Thoughts of Kierkegaard
W.H. AUDEN W.H. Auden's Book of Light Verse
ERICH AUERBACH Dante: Poet of the Secular World
EVE BABITZ Eve's Hollywood*
EVE BABITZ Slow Days, Fast Company: The World, the Flesh, and L.A.*
DOROTHY BAKER Cassandra at the Wedding*
DOROTHY BAKER Young Man with a Horn*
J.A. BAKER The Peregrine
HONORÉ DE BALZAC The Human Comedy: Selected Stories*
HONORÉ DE BALZAC The Unknown Masterpiece *and* Gambara*
VICKI BAUM Grand Hotel*
SYBILLE BEDFORD A Favorite of the Gods *and* A Compass Error*
SYBILLE BEDFORD A Legacy*
SYBILLE BEDFORD A Visit to Don Otavio: A Mexican Journey*
MAX BEERBOHM The Prince of Minor Writers: The Selected Essays of Max Beerbohm*
STEPHEN BENATAR Wish Her Safe at Home*
FRANS G. BENGTSSON The Long Ships*
ALEXANDER BERKMAN Prison Memoirs of an Anarchist
GEORGES BERNANOS Mouchette
MIRON BIAŁOSZEWSKI A Memoir of the Warsaw Uprising*
ADOLFO BIOY CASARES Asleep in the Sun
ADOLFO BIOY CASARES The Invention of Morel
PAUL BLACKBURN (TRANSLATOR) Proensa*
CAROLINE BLACKWOOD Corrigan*
CAROLINE BLACKWOOD Great Granny Webster*
RONALD BLYTHE Akenfield: Portrait of an English Village*
NICOLAS BOUVIER The Way of the World
EMMANUEL BOVE Henri Duchemin and His Shadows*
MALCOLM BRALY On the Yard*
MILLEN BRAND The Outward Room*
ROBERT BRESSON Notes on the Cinematograph*
SIR THOMAS BROWNE Religio Medici and Urne-Buriall*

* *Also available as an electronic book.*